LOVE YOU, LOVEDAY

G.A.HAUSER

First G.A. Hauser publication: February 2010

Chapter One

"Hey, Oliver! Come over here."

His books under his arm, Oliver Loveday approached Perry Brooks in the chaos in-between classes. "What do you want? I've got to get to biology class."

"You never told me your old man used to be a porn star."

Oliver cringed in reflex. "He wasn't a porn star. He just did some movies in the Eighties, that's all." He noticed a pimple about to pop on Perry's greasy chin.

"Yeah, right," Perry snickered. "He had sex in them, Oliver. I hate to inform you, but that means he's a porn star, dude."

"Shut up. Leave me alone." Looking over his shoulder as he hurried to his class, Oliver endured Perry's smirk until he turned a corner in the hall.

He set his books down on his desk and collapsed in the chair. Oliver felt sick. No one was supposed to find out. How the heck had Perry?

Gabriel "Angel" Loveday arranged the fiction novels in his bookshop, The Uncut Buzzard, in alphabetical order on the shelf. A shipment had arrived of the latest best sellers he had hand-picked off the list. The carton open at his feet, he slipped the new arrivals into the slots while his assistant, Summer

Thompson, helped a customer at the counter. When she was finished ringing up the sale, she stood behind Angel to see what new stock had come in.

"Oooh! These look interesting. Lee Rowan? GA Hauser? New authors?"

Pausing to investigate one of the slick cover designs, Angel replied, "Yeah, I thought our gay erotica could use some beefing up. It's looking a little sparse at the moment."

"Cool!" She added the one in her hand to its place on the shelf. "Is that the entire shipment or is there more in back?"

"No. This is it for now." He removed the last book from the carton, then flattened the cardboard box.

"I think we can get rid if that 'back to school' display and begin setting out some Halloween stuff. What do you think?" Summer mused out loud.

Checking his watch like it would tell the season, Angel shook his head and muttered, "Where the hell's the time gone? It can't be Halloween already."

"Just about, hot stuff!" Summer giggled, heading over to the table where the schoolbooks were set out.

Smiling to himself at her enthusiasm, Angel brought the cardboard to the back door to put out with the rest of the garbage. When he had set it down, he sighed tiredly, took the elastic band off his long ponytail, and shook out his straight brown hair so he could rub his fingers over his scalp to try and wake up. It was only an hour 'til closing time and he wondered how Oliver had done in school.

Shelving a stack of reference books, Summer watched Angel return to the counter to serve a customer. Angel had taken the ribbon out of his hair and it flowed down past his shoulders in long, straight locks. She admired his height, over six feet tall, and his incredible slender build. Clean-shaven with the most brilliant blue eyes she had ever seen in a man, she couldn't help but flirt with the guy even though he had ten years on her. He was amazing looking. It was because of Angel that she loved her job, loved coming to this cozy little bookshop snuggled between a café and a mystic crystal shop, loved the view across the street of the Pacific Ocean, the smell of sea and sand every time the door opened and that little bell jingled to announce another customer. Redondo Beach was a long way from Manhattan Island, but she loved the area and she never looked back. Working closely with Angel, she had noticed something sad and mysterious to him. She wondered why. It intrigued her. Maybe that was what kept her interested.

Angel thanked the young man for his purchase and watched him leave the shop; the chime made a little tinkle sound as the door swung open and closed again. After the customer vanished, Angel approached Summer to see what she was up to. "Linus and Snoopy next to Poe and Rice? That's strangely juxtaposed even for your tastes."

Setting up a small cardboard cutout of the Peanuts characters in a pumpkin patch, Summer replied, "You can't argue with the Great Pumpkin, Angel. Sorry."

"Where did you find that display?" He picked it up to inspect.

"In the cubbyhole in the back room. You wouldn't believe the stuff that's in there."

"Must be from the previous owner. I don't remember buying this one." He set it back down on the table.

"Are you and Oliver coming to my Halloween party?" Summer shouted from behind a shelf.

Trying not to grimace at the thought of a costume party, Angel didn't answer. When Summer came back to where he stood he was still gazing at Snoopy and Linus wistfully.

"Angel? Hello?" She laughed. "You are coming. You have to come."

"Uh…" He tried to think up a good excuse.

"Don't be like that!" She hit his arm playfully. "Do something exciting for once."

Raising his eyebrows at the comment, Angel didn't even want to discuss his past "exciting" life with her, to tell her he'd had enough "excitement" to last him a lifetime. She didn't need to know. No one did. It was almost twenty years ago. No one remembered those old movies anyway.

"You're going," she warned. "I won't take no for an answer."

"Do I have to dress up? I hate dressing up."

"Yes! Angel!"

Holding up his hands to fend off the attack, Angel just smiled at her persistence. He noticed another customer standing at the counter to purchase a book. After he rung up the sale, he sighed tiredly and stared out at the white sand and the tranquil beach. Some days he wished he could erase everything he'd done in the past, and some days he appreciated it for giving him the money he needed to open up his bookstore. As long as the past stayed buried, he could live with it.

"Hey, Loveday!"

Oliver stopped in his tracks on his walk to the bus. Seeing who was shouting his name, he grumbled, "What do you want?"

Perry sauntered over to him, his spiked hair not moving an inch in the warm breeze. "One of the guys said you play guitar."

"So?"

"You know Len Parks?"

"Yeah, what about him?" Oliver replied.

"He plays drums. You want to form a band?" Perry glanced back over his shoulder, then asked, "What are you looking at?"

"My bus. I don't want to miss it."

"I can give you a ride."

"Oh. Okay. Anything's better than the bus. It takes forever." Oliver followed Perry to where he had parked his jeep. As he climbed into the passenger side, Oliver said, "Nice wheels. Your parents buy it for you?"

"Yeah." Perry started the engine.

Oliver felt slightly jealous. His father didn't exactly have the funds to finance a new car for him after investing all his savings in their house and the bookshop. "I live just south of—"

"I know where you live," Perry sneered.

"Oh." Oliver set his book bag down on the floor in front of him and tried not to stare at Perry's profile. The boy was ugly. Oliver didn't think of himself as a great beauty, but he knew he had to be better looking that that! He felt sorry for Perry. His skin was a mess; his hair had been coated with so much gel it stood up stiff as nails, from his scalp. In contrast to the red acne, Perry's already pale complexion appeared even more pallid. Perry's paunch added to the combination. For a seventeen year old, he was fat. Oliver imagined the only exercise he endured involved moving his thumbs over a video game control. "How do you know where I live, Per?" Oliver gazed out of the window as they drove northbound.

"I Googled your last name. All sorts of shit came up. Not about you…but about your dad. Is Angel Loveday his real name or is it something they made up for him when he stared in those x-rated movies?"

Trying not to get upset and knowing he couldn't battle with every person who figured it out, Oliver exhaled a deep breath. "His real name is Gabriel Loveday. Angel is just a nickname his mom gave him when he was young. They weren't x-rated, Per. They were just like R or something. He told me they were art-house films. You know. Not like real porn." Hearing a condescending snicker from Perry, Oliver turned to look at him finally. "If you think it's funny, why the hell do you want to hang around with me?"

5

"I don't think it's funny. I think it's cool."

"Oh." That disarmed Oliver completely. "I suppose it is kind of cool. I don't ask him about it much. He's not really keen on talking about it."

"You ever see any of those old movies? Like *Filth*?"

"*Filth*?" Oliver tried to decide if that rang a bell.

"Yeah. That was the name of his first movie. Don't you even know about the stupid movies he made? If my dad was that cool, I'd know everything about it." Perry pulled into the dirt and gravel driveway of Oliver's beachfront home.

Oliver was still trying to get over the name of the film. Suddenly he felt a little too protected by his dad. "Thanks, Per." Oliver made a move to climb out.

"Ah, can I come in for a minute?"

"Why?"

"Have to take a leak."

"Oh. Okay." Oliver hopped out of the jeep and led the way to his front door. He checked the time, aware his father would be coming home soon. He usually closed the bookstore at four o'clock so he could make dinner for them.

Using his key, Oliver unlocked the door and stepped inside the very modest two-bedroom home. There were only four rooms in total, including the bathroom. What it lacked in grandeur it made up on location. Looking over the sparse furnishings, Oliver tried to see the interior with fresh eyes. Oliver knew Perry came from money and apologized, "I know it's not much, but the backyard view is fantastic."

"Is it?"

"Yeah. Come here." Oliver led him through the living room to the back door. Opening it for him, they entered a small screen-enclosed porch and then moved onto a sandy patch of grass beyond it. As they stepped outside, the wind blew Oliver's long hair back from his face. "Check it out."

Perry stood still a moment, as if absorbing the view. Then he approached the edge of what appeared to be a drop in the land.

Walking with him to the end, Oliver said, "There's a ladder Dad made that you can climb down to get to the actual beach." Perry nodded in reply, inspecting it. Oliver added, "He said we should have some kind of fence here, you know, to stop someone from toppling off at night, but I don't think he's ever going to build it. I mean, it's just us here, and we know where the edge is."

"There's something I don't get." Perry moved away from the drop, as if he was nervous about being so near to it.

"What?"

"How come he has a son when he's gay? And where's your mom?"

Feeling insulted by Perry's blunt, nosy questions, Oliver muttered, "I thought you had to pee."

"Yeah, I do. But I just have to know why. I mean, he did things to guys in those movies, Oliver."

It was something else Oliver hadn't been privy to. Maybe by protecting him, his dad was really just keeping him ignorant.

Like a pit-bull with a piece of meat, Perry moved closer, obviously not willing to let it go. "What happened to your mom, Oliver?"

"She died." Oliver bit his lip sadly.

"Of what?"

"Cancer. She died when I was seven." Oliver returned to the house, pausing in the porch to take off his sandy shoes.

"So, your dad is bi then?"

"I don't know! Why does it mean so much to you?" Oliver shouted, getting annoyed.

"It doesn't. Just curious. Where's the bathroom?"

"There." Oliver nodded to a door. After Perry vanished

into it, Oliver glanced over at some framed photos that were set up on the mantelpiece. They were of his entire family, the three of them: his dad, his mom, and him.

Angel pulled into his driveway, noticing a strange jeep there. Parking along side it so it could get out without him moving his car, he wondered who Oliver had brought home. Carrying groceries that he had purchase on the way, he found the front door unlocked and pushed it back. "Oliver?"

When his son spun around, the look of mistrust in Oliver's eyes surprised him. "You okay?" Angel set the groceries down on the kitchen table. "Who's here with you?" Just as he spoke those words, a very strange looking teenager emerged from the bathroom. Though the appearance of the boy upset Angel, he tried to be polite. "Who's your new friend?"

"This is Perry, Dad." Oliver's pout didn't fade.

"Hello, Perry." Angel tried to make it sound friendly, though he had no idea what his handsome son was doing with such an odd character.

"Hello, Mr. Loveday," Perry sang strangely, smirking.

After getting an intimidating inspection, which included his groin area, Angel pointed to the kitchen as an excuse to leave the room. "I have groceries to unpack." As he filled the cabinets and refrigerator with his purchases, he heard Oliver say, "So, thanks for the lift, Per. See ya tomorrow in school?"

"Yeah. Think about the band, Oliver. Len is really pumped about it, and all we need is you on guitar."

"Okay. I'll talk to Len tomorrow in class. He never mentioned it to me before."

"He wanted me to ask you first."

"Oh. Okay."

Angel peeked out of the kitchen and found Oliver had walked Perry to the door. When Perry met his eyes, Angel almost flinched at the connection he made, as if it were satanic in nature.

"Nice meeting you, Mr. Loveday," he sang again.

"Yeah, see ya, Perry." Angel couldn't even force a smile.

When he left, Angel sighed with relief. A loaf of bread in his hands while he unpacked the shopping bags, he shouted to Oliver, "Where the hell did you find him?"

"Forget it, Dad," Oliver yelled back, then closed himself into his bedroom.

In the silence that followed, Angel shivered in exaggeration and mumbled, "Ew, creepy kid..."

Chapter Two

Angel opened the bookshop door and deactivated the alarm. Just as he was closing it, he noticed Summer hurrying to catch him.

"Good morning, Angel," she chirped cheerfully.

"Hiya, Summer." He opened the door wider to allow her to pass inside.

"Should I get our usual lattes from next door?" she shouted as she went to set her purse in the office.

"Sure." Angel met her in the back room to get her some money.

"I got it." She waved his hand away.

"Take it out of petty cash."

"Don't worry about it." She removed a five dollar bill out of her wallet, then met Angel's eyes. "You okay?"

"Hmm?" He snapped back into focus. "Yeah, look, you know we take our coffee money from the cash box. Don't pay for it out of your own." He opened a small metal container that rested on his desk and handed her some bills. When Angel didn't hear a reply, he glanced up. Summer was smiling brightly at him. "What?" he asked curiously.

"You are the best boss!"

When she jumped on him for a hug, he reacted in surprise.

"Okay, lady, get going."

Breaking the embrace, Summer beamed at him, purring, "Wow, was it as good for you as it was for me?"

"Go get the coffees, you silly girl." He blushed, very flattered to still be seen as attractive to a beautiful woman in her twenties.

"Be right back!" Summer waved the money and jogged out of the office excitedly.

Amused by her upbeat energy, Angel knelt down by the safe to get out the money for the cash register. The happy sentiment falling to a frown, Angel began recalling the conversation he had with his son last night over dinner. Though they hadn't seen it necessary to bring it up before, other than just in passing, last night Oliver was digging at him for details. How many movies did he make? What were the names? Did he really have sex with men in them?

The discussion had upset Angel terribly, and the defensive attitude from his son gnawed at him. Why, after sixteen years of no interest, did Oliver suddenly have to know all the sordid details? It wasn't fair. The poor boy shouldn't be burdened with such a father.

The tinkling sound of the door chime reached his ears. Angel checked his watch. It was still too early for customers, so Angel assumed it was Summer returning with the coffees. Counting out the money in the cash drawer to place into the register, Angel was surprised it was taking so long for Summer to come back to the office. When the sound of the chime echoed through the shop once more, he stood up to have a look. He did a quick scan around the small room, finding no one. Deciding the noise was from the wind, Angel shrugged his shoulders indifferently and returned to his office with the intention of bringing the cash drawer to the counter.

Before he made it there, Summer passed by the large glass front window on her way back. Angel smiled, cherishing the days they spent together. She was like his best friend, his sister.

11

He adored her.

Knowing they had a little bit of time before the shop opened to the public, Angel set the cash drawer back down on his desk and waited as Summer brought him his double-shot latte. "Mmm, smells great. Thanks, sweetie."

"My pleasure. Here's your change."

"Just stick it back into the petty cash box."

She nodded, tossing the coins in. "Oh, is that ready for the till?" She pointed to the drawer.

"Yes. I was just bringing it up to the counter."

"I can do it." She set her coffee down on his desk.

"Okay. Thanks. Don't open yet. Give us five minutes to drink our coffee."

"Okay!"

As she carried the cash drawer to the front of the shop where the counter was located, Angel decided to bring her coffee with him so they could stare out at the beach together as they sipped them.

Right after she shut the cash register drawer with the newly loaded cash in it, Angel heard her exclaim, "What the heck is that?"

"What's what?" He approached her and noticed her staring at the glass counter top.

Just as Angel set her coffee down, Summer held up a video. When Angel read the title and made out the photo on the cover, he died inside.

"Is this you?" Summer asked in excitement. "Angel? Oh, my god! It is you! You were in a movie? *Filth*? You were in a movie named *Filth*? Look at you. You're gorgeous! Oh, I don't believe this. Why didn't you ever tell me you were in a movie?"

He felt sick. An icy feeling washed over his skin as if he had fallen into a cold pool. "Where did you get that?"

"It was here." She pointed to the counter. "I need to watch

this tonight. Man, are you incredible!"

"No!" He lunged for it.

Moving it out of his reach, Summer giggled wickedly. "Uh uh, no way. I'm going to see you in action, you gorgeous god you."

"No. Come on, Summer. It was a long time ago. It's too embarrassing."

Hearing her wild laughter as she raced to hide it from him in the back room, he rubbed his forehead tiredly, then looked at the front door. Who the hell would come in and leave that video on the counter? It didn't make sense.

Trying to convince Summer not to watch the video was like trying to convince a toddler not to have a tantrum. Impossible. The uneasiness of his past being revealed permeated Angel's mood throughout the day. Maybe he shouldn't be so sensitive about it. Other people had made worse movies. His weren't even considered pornography in the truest sense of the word. No. It wasn't an hour of shoving dicks into holes. His movies had plots, storylines; they were avant-garde, artistic. Or at least that's what the director called them. Plimpton. Buster Plimpton. His name was synonymous with camp Eighties era films.

"You okay?"

Angel raised his head from his paperwork to see Summer's pensive smile. "Yeah."

"You shouldn't be ashamed, Angel. You're lucky you got the chance to be a star. Most guys around here don't get that chance."

Setting his pen down, looking at his watch, Angel asked, "Are we still open?"

"No. I locked up."

Nodding, Angel stretched his arms over his head, arching his back from being seated too long.

13

"Why are you so sensitive about it, Angel?"

Chuckling sadly as he rested his elbows on the desk in front of him, Angel replied, "It's not like I was Cary Grant, Summer. Not exactly Oscar winning performances."

"So? Big deal. They still make you immortal. Someone somewhere has those movies and you will forever be remembered."

"Really?" he replied sarcastically. "You didn't have a clue who I was when I hired you. And I was glad. Believe me."

"Yeah, but, I'm young. I bet people your age all know who you are." She sat down on the corner of his desk.

"Ouch. Was that meant to be a compliment?" He peeked up at her sheepishly.

Her expression suddenly became one of seduction. Leaning closer, she cupped his jaw and whispered, "I don't care how old you are, Angel Loveday. I think you're incredibly attractive."

Slowly moving her hands back from his face, Angel replied, "And coming from someone who can easily do a spread in Playboy, it's either an amazing compliment or pity on the old boy."

"Stop it! You think I would be attracted to you if I didn't think you were...well, attractive? Sexy? Built like a—"

"Okay...let's not get carried away." He held up his hand.

"No. Let's get carried away."

Standing up, backing away from her, Angel chided, "Ms. Thompson, don't. We've had a very good working relationship up to now."

A stunned look crossed her face. "You really don't want to touch me?"

Imagining another man most certainly jumping at the chance, Angel mumbled, "I don't. I'm sorry."

"Wow. Maybe it's my turn to feel upset." She stood up off the desk and straightened her blouse nervously, as if it wasn't perfectly tucked in.

"No. Don't be. Look, I wasn't going to tell you any of this because it didn't seem to matter, and it's certainly not come up before this, but...I prefer men to women."

"Huh? For real? No way. But you have a son."

"I do. And I was even married for a short while. It still doesn't change my preference, Summer. I'm sorry."

"It's okay, Angel. Believe me. I don't care. Of course I would love to get you into my bed, but I do understand. I won't put you into this situation again, okay, boss?"

He smiled in relief. "Thank you. Okay. Time to go home."

"I'll get the cash for the safe."

"Thanks." As she left the office, Angel felt guilty for not returning her advance, but he knew how he felt deep inside his heart. He didn't want another heterosexual relationship. Feeling the pangs of loneliness because, for his son's sake, he hadn't been with a man in over a decade, he muttered sadly, "From fucking like a bunny to celibacy. I have a very strange life." He released a deep sigh from his chest as he finished closing up the shop.

When he came through the door of his cottage, Angel called out, "Oliver!" but didn't hear a response. Tossing his keys on the counter, he knocked on Oliver's bedroom door lightly, then pushed it open to see inside. Oliver was seated at his computer, his back facing Angel. "Why didn't you answer me when I called your name?" Walking up behind Oliver, Angel looked at the images on the screen and choked in shock. "Oliver! What the hell are you doing?"

"What's wrong, Dad?" he said dryly. "Can't stand to see yourself naked?"

"Shut it off!" Angel reached for the power button.

Oliver blocked his hand. "Look, Dad! Look at the proud legacy you've created for our family history."

"Why are you doing this?" Angel groaned.

"I had no idea there was so much about you out there on the internet until Perry enlightened me. Check this one out, Dad; there's you sucking a man's dick. And another one of you naked, rubbing oil on another guy…and another one—"

"Oliver!" Angel shouted. "Close down that site!"

"Why?" Oliver spun his chair around to confront him. "Are you embarrassed, Dad? So embarrassed that you neglected to tell me what you have done in your past so that I had to hear it from a classmate? You know, not knowing was almost worse than what you did for a living back then." He turned back to the images, adding, "No. I take it back. Not worse than what you did. Geezuz! Are you gay?"

Angel felt trapped. Trapped by his own past, his own reality. Moving as if he were numb, Angel dropped to sit on his son's bed, avoiding looking at those incriminating photos. "I'm sorry, Oliver."

"You should be! Did Mom know? Did she know what you did when she met you?"

"Yes."

"And she married you anyway? What the hell was she thinking?"

"Come on, Oliver, give me a break. I was only eighteen years old when I did those movies."

"Oh? Is that your excuse? So in two years I can go make porno films?"

Rubbing his face, Angel knew any excuse was going to defeat him. He turned to see his son's expression, trying to ignore the image on the computer screen behind him. "It was different back then. Your grandfather and I were at odds. He kicked me out of the house, Oliver. I had to make money somehow."

"By screwing guys on a movie set?"

"It wasn't like that. Those photos aren't a true depiction of the movies I did. Scenes like that were rare in them. It was usually just one in the end. It wasn't like real porno films…" Angel groaned in anguish. "I don't believe I'm having to explain this same shit to justify my life to my own son. It's what I've been doing for the last twenty years. I've had to constantly go over and over this with everyone and I'm sick to death of it. Oliver, just shut off the damn computer and forget you ever found it."

"Oh, sure, Dad. I'll just go on pretending my father is normal."

Angel grew sick of the nude shots of himself. He stormed over to the desk and reached under it to unplug the power. Throwing down the end of the cord angrily, he stood back up and hissed, "Don't make this an issue between us, Oliver. We need each other. We have no one else to depend on."

"Is that why I never see my grandparents?" he accused.

"No! They're just busy people."

"Liar!"

"Oliver, they don't hold any of this against you. Call your grandfather. Go ahead. He'll come see you."

"I should! I should go live with them!" Oliver stood up, as if he were threatening to leave.

"I'm sorry, okay?" Angel threw up his hands in frustration. "I did the best I could back then. I was young and stupid. Some guy offered me a huge amount of money, Oliver. And at eighteen I knew I couldn't make that kind of dough any other way. But, they are not porn. They are art-house films. I never would have done a porn film."

Oliver's mouth hung open as if what he was hearing was unbelievable. Finally he spoke softly, "I don't know what planet you're from, Dad, but when you strip naked and screw someone on film, it's porno."

"No. You're wrong. Look at the movies out now. Come on, Oliver, there's sex in all of them."

"They don't show a guy's penis! Dad, I'm not an idiot. Stop treating me like one."

Angel couldn't stand it anymore. Leaving the room, he headed to the back of the house and opened the door to the ocean breeze. Over two decades ago he had these same arguments with his father, almost identical in nature, and he was sick to death of defending his actions.

Kicking off his shoes and socks, Angel crossed the grassy lawn, then climbed down the home-made ladder to sea level. Twilight was already tingeing the sky with pink and lavender hues as the sun set. Walking out to the tide, he felt the cold damp sand between his toes and tried to find some peace. For twenty years he had been able to forget his past. Why was it all coming up to the surface now? Why?

When the phone rang, Oliver thought about letting the answering machine pick it up, then answered it. "Hello?"

"Geez, finally. Why were you on the phone for so long?"

"Oh, hi, Perry. I wasn't. I was on the net."

"Don't you have broadband?"

"No."

"Did you find anything good?"

"I can't believe you were right. There are a ton of sites with naked pictures of my dad. How embarrassing is that?"

"I still think it's cool."

"Gross! He sucked a guy's cock, Per! I can't even look him in the face." Oliver stared back at the entrance to his room. Hearing nothing at the other end, Oliver asked, "You still there?"

"Yeah. I'm looking at the site now."

"What? What site?"

"That one I told you about. With all your dad's films on them."

"Why do you want to look at those pictures, Perry? I wish you never told me about them." Again Perry didn't reply. Oliver tried to hear more clearly over the line. "You still there?"

"Yeah…"

"You keep sounding like you're not there. What are you doing?" Oliver listened more closely. A grunting noise reached him. "Perry?"

"Yeah…"

"What the heck's going on? You still checking out those stupid websites?"

"Yeah…he's on them. Christ, he has a big dick."

"You're not funny, Per. Anyway, forget those stupid things." He heard some more rustling sounds over the phone and couldn't imagine what Perry was up to. "You still there? What the heck are you doing? It sounds like you're taking a piss or something."

A wicked chuckle was followed by the sound of a zipper, then Perry hissed, "No, not taking a piss. Anyway, we still on for tomorrow?"

"Oh. I forgot to ask my dad about that." Oliver reclined back on his bed.

"You think he'll care?"

"No. Just come over. He wouldn't dare say no now."

"Okay. See ya tomorrow at about ten. Len's coming by as well."

"Cool. I'll see ya then." Oliver hung up, looked over at the blank screen of his computer, then climbed off the bed to find his father.

Angel was just walking back to the house after a long stroll down the beach. The light was fading to darkness and he couldn't see very well in front of him. Only a sliver of the moon was showing in the starry sky. Finding the rickety ladder, he climbed up, the sound of sand falling around him from the sheer sides, and stood on the house level brushing off the gritty specks from his arms and feet. When he moved towards the back door, he realized Oliver was there waiting for him. Inhaling for courage, Angel approached him, checking out Oliver's expression. "Am I forgiven?"

A sad smile emerged on Oliver's face. "Yeah, I suppose."

"Thanks, Oliver. It means a lot to me." Angel put his arm around his son's shoulder and walked inside with him. "Now, what are you hungry for? Shall I call for a pizza?"

"Pepperoni?"

"You got it." Angel smiled brightly.

Chapter Three

Saturday morning, the sound of the garage door opening brought Angel out of his slumber. Curious as to why someone was in the garage at that hour, he climbed out of bed, slipped a pair of jeans on, and headed out front to investigate.

Oliver was wheeling Angel's motorcycle out onto the driveway.

"What are you doing?" Angel asked.

"A couple of guys are coming by to practice in a band."

"Oh? And this is the first I'm hearing about it?" Angel crossed his arms over his bare chest.

"It was a last minute decision. Just three of us, Dad. It's no big deal. There's no room in the house for Len's drums, so I have to make room out here."

"Since when did you become interested in a band?" Angel helped him pile some boxes out of the way.

Oliver shrugged. "You have to work, right?"

"Yeah, 'til four. Why?"

"No reason."

"Oliver," Angel admonished. "Why? What are you guys going to do that you don't want me knowing about?"

"Nothing!"

"Fine. Be that way, Oliver. I really can't stand the wall

you're putting up between us." Angel brushed off his hands and returned to the front door. As he did he heard his son mutter, "You think you're the only one who can have secrets?"

Trying not to turn it into an argument, Angel headed to the shower. As he removed his clothing he pretended he had faith in his son.

Sweating from the effort of clearing a space for them to practice, Oliver heard the sound of a car pulling into his drive. He poked his head out of the garage and spotted the jeep. Whiping his hands on his jeans, Oliver waved as he spied Perry behind the wheel. Once Perry had shut off the engine, he climbed out and walked towards Oliver.

"Hey, Per. How's it going?"

"Okay. Uh, is your dad here?"

"He's inside. He's working today so we can have the place to ourselves."

Perry nodded, looking back at the house. "Can I use the bathroom?"

Oliver gaped at him. "Again? Do you have a piss problem or something?"

"Too much coffee, dude."

Shaking his head in amazement, Oliver pointed over his shoulder. "Go inside."

Perry nodded in reply and jogged to the front door.

A pick-up truck pulled in behind Perry's jeep. Oliver waved at Len, and approached the window of Len's truck. "Hey, Lenny, you need a hand with your drums?"

"Yeah. Thanks, Oliver. I see Perry's car. Where the hell is he?" Len looked around the front of the house and garage.

"Inside takin' a leak. The guy pisses constantly. He's always asking to use the damn toilet."

Len cracked up with laughter, then opened the door of his

truck. "He thinks he can sing, Oliver. This I gotta see."

Oliver grinned in amusement at Len's expression as he helped him unload his drums. After they had them set up the garage, Oliver noticed Perry just coming over to join them. "What the heck took you so long?"

"Constipated. Sorry. Double-flusher."

Len and Oliver exchanged grimaces, not commenting.

Wrapping a towel around his waist, Angel left the bathroom and headed to his room to dress. After closing the door to his bedroom, he tossed the towel on the bed and dug through his drawers for some clothing to wear. Checking the time on his watch, he swore under his breath at how late it had become and rushed to slip on a pair of jeans and a cotton shirt. As he was tucking in his shirt, he found his closet door was open and moved to shut it before he left. Just before he did he noticed some of his clothing had fallen to the floor. Thinking it odd, he began grabbing his shirts to hang back up, cursed again under his breath at how late he was getting, and decided to deal with it when he returned home that afternoon. Kicking the rest of the clothing back inside the closet, he closed the door and then rushed out to grab his keys.

As he stepped out of the house he heard the pounding of a drum beat coming from the garage. Pausing to take a look inside, Angel found his son sitting on a chair tuning his guitar, a kid with a shaved head banging on the drums, and Perry standing in front of them both with a cordless microphone in his hand. The moment Angel showed up, the three of them stopped what they were doing and stared at him.

"Sorry." Angel waved for them to continue, "I didn't mean to disturb you."

"Hey, Dad," Oliver shouted, then pointed behind his shoulder. "That's Len."

"Hi, Len." Angel smiled, then caught Perry's strange sneer.

23

Seeing his son was watching him, Angel mumbled hello to the pointy-haired kid, then addressed his son again. "I'm heading out. You going to be okay?"

"Yeah, why wouldn't I be?" Oliver laughed sarcastically, rolling his eyes at his two friends.

After glancing over at Perry's unnerving stare, Angel replied, "All right. You know how to contact me if you need me. See you later."

Perry sang, "Bye, Mr. Loveday."

Angel didn't respond to it, just gave Oliver a last nod of his head before he left. Once Angel was in his car, he cringed at leaving that eerie kid near his son.

Parking in his usual spot behind the shop next to Summer's Mazda, Angel hurried his pace, checking his watch again. When he turned the corner of the building, he found her sipping her latte, waiting. "Shit. I'm sorry, Summer. I was running late." He opened the door for her and disarmed the security alarm. "I should get you a key. I have no idea why you don't have one."

"It's okay, Angel. No big deal. I have your latte. I just hope it's still hot."

"You're a doll. Thanks." He took it from her as he walked to the back office. After he had set it on the desk Angel raised his head to see Summer smiling strangely at him. "Something wrong?"

"I watched that movie last night. Oh-my-God," she crooned.

"Oh." He averted his eyes from her ogling stare and got busy.

"Angel Loveday, you are a god! A G-O-D!"

"Cut it out. Let's not get carried away." He crouched down to open the safe.

Sitting on the desk, sipping her coffee, Summer whispered,

"Do you have any other movies I can borrow?"

Knowing he had them all hidden away in his closet at home, Angel didn't answer right away. Once he had the cash out of the safe, he stood up and faced her, seeing her wicked grin. "I won't hear the end of it now, will I?"

"No! Angel, you've nothing to be ashamed of. On the contrary. Those movies were so hot I was squirming in my seat watching them. They got me really horny."

"Too much information!" Angel held up his hand to stop her, sitting down behind the desk to get the till ready for opening.

As she leaned closer, she spoke softly. "I was insanely jealous of those men you were with."

"All right..." Angel chided but smiled at the compliment.

"You are beautiful, Angel Loveday. Don't ever think that you're not. Okay?"

"Okay. Thanks, Summer. Can we stop talking about it now?"

"Okay, boss!" She hopped off the desk and got busy in the shop.

When she left, Angel's gaze unfocused as he remembered that era of his life. It was an amazing experience to have done it, but he just wished it would go back undercover and leave him to move on.

Angel felt more weary than usual on his journey home. Seeing his driveway was devoid of strange cars, he exhaled with relief and pulled in. As his car faced the front of his house he noticed his motorcycle was still outside. Annoyed that Oliver hadn't wheeled it back into the garage, Angel parked his Camaro and headed to the front door. When he poked his head inside, he shouted, "Oliver!" No sound returned. "Oliver?" He walked to Oliver's room and found it empty.

Muttering in irritation under his breath, Angel went back

outside and opened the garage to take care of the job himself. Once the bike had been returned to its place, Angel had a quick look around, then shut the garage door and made his way back inside the house again. On his way through the living room he looked for a note of some kind as to where Oliver had gone, found none, and headed to his room to drop off his wallet and keys on his dresser.

The moment he entered his bedroom, he noticed his closet door was open again. Tilting his head curiously, he wondered what Oliver would be doing, going through his things. Moving closer, Angel looked inside his closet, seeing his clothing still piled on the floor. Sighing tiredly, he picked up the shirts that had lain there since morning, to hang back up on their hangers. As he crouched down, he found a box that was stored behind his clothing was also open, the flaps unfolded and sticking up. He knew inside that crate were some of his old videos and memorabilia from that forgotten time. "Great. Now that Oliver knows about the films he's digging for them." Taking the box completely out of the closet so he could inspect it, he knew immediately that some of his movies were missing. "Oliver!" he shouted in anger. Fuming at the invasion of privacy, Angel knew if Oliver had asked to see them, he would have shown them to him. But sneaking behind his back? That was low, and it was out of character for his honest son.

Flapping the box closed again, Angel pushed it to the back of the closet where it belonged, then rose up to resume setting his shirts on their hangers. He picked one cotton shirt up off the bed, pausing to stare at it. "What the fuck?" A white milky stain spattered the material. He knew what it looked like immediately, but his rational brain was trying to come up with another explanation. Reluctantly he took a sniff. "I don't believe this." He threw the entire pile of shirts into the laundry basket, and carried it to the laundry room to put into the washing machine in disgust.

Just as he was loading the washer, he heard the front door opening. Tossing in the powder and turning the machine on first, Angel then hunted for his son. He found him kicking off his shoes in his bedroom.

"Oh. Hi, Dad."

"What were you doing in my closet?"

"Huh?" Oliver sat down on his bed.

"You heard me. What were you doing snooping inside my closet while I was gone? If you have any questions about those movies, ask me."

"You're mental," Oliver choked sarcastically, lying back on the bed so he wasn't facing him any longer.

"What the hell's gotten into you? Since when do you lie to me about a simple question?"

"I'm not lying!" Oliver shouted in defense. "You're the one who's losing it."

"Well, if you weren't…" Angel paused as the words were coming out of his mouth. "Wait a minute…you had friends over. Were they in the house?"

"Yeah, why?"

"You let your friends go into my room, Oliver?"

"No!" Oliver crossed his arms tightly over his chest.

Angel tried not to scream, but he was furious. "Was it Perry? Was Perry in my room?"

"He used the bathroom, that's all. Leave me alone. I'm sick and tired of arguing with you."

When Oliver rolled over so his back was facing Angel, Angel left the room and headed to the rear of the house to stare at the crashing waves. He didn't know what was going on, but whatever it was he wasn't happy about it.

Chapter Four

Monday morning Angel was back at work, busy with customers and trying not to be too distracted about the strange wall of silence Oliver had erected between them.

When noon approached, Angel asked Summer, "What do you want from next door?"

"Ah, how about just a garden salad and a roll," she replied as she tidied up the shelves after a hectic morning rush of customers.

"I'll be right back." Angel headed outside to walk next door to the café. The scent of baking bread and coffee filled his nostrils as he opened the door. A line had formed, so he stood patiently deciding on what to eat. When his turn came he smiled warmly at the woman behind the counter. "Hello, Mary."

"Hello, Angel, what can I get you today?"

"How about a garden salad and a roll for Summer and a club sandwich for me?"

"Coming right up!" Mary smiled sweetly and began preparing his order. As she did she asked, "Busy today, Angel?"

"Yes, swamped. How about you?"

"Yes, we were really busy this morning. I was surprised at all the foot traffic."

Nodding in agreement, Angel looked outside the large glass front window and admired the same view his shop shared.

Someone had been standing in front of it and quickly lowered their heads and hurried away when he made eye contact. Angel felt his skin crawl. "Perry?" he said to himself. Seeing Mary was still busy preparing the food, Angel jogged to the door to look out. No one resembling that freak was in the area. Checking the time curiously, Angel knew Perry should have been in school and began doubting what he had seen. Hearing Mary shouting his name, he returned to the counter and removed his wallet from his back pocket.

"Is everything okay, Angel?" Mary asked in concern.

Knowing he was most likely expressing his frustration, Angel forced a smile and handed her some cash. "Everything's fine, Mary. Just fine."

Summer was helping a customer at the Health and Wellness section of the shop when he returned. Passing by them quickly, Angel set their food on his desk in the office and walked back out to the shop in case someone needed help at the cash register. Just as he was making his way across the sales floor, an elderly woman asked him, "Do you work here?"

"Yes, I do." He listened to her request regarding a book on travel. "I have one here that's a Planet Earth series. It has everything you need to know about a trip to Hawaii." Angel handed it to her.

"Oh, that's perfect! How much is it?"

Angel took it back from her and read the price. "Nine-ninety-five, but I'll give it to you for eight. How's that?"

"That's very kind of you."

He carried it to the counter for her to ring up. His attention on the cash register keys, Angel heard her exclaim in surprise. Distracted by the sound of her gasp, he twisted towards her and asked, "Are you okay?"

When she didn't answer, Angel looked down to where she was gawking. A naked photo of him rested on the glass top of the counter. Instantly he grabbed it and pushed it to the floor behind him. "Uh, that's eight-sixty-four total including tax." The blush burning his cheeks, Angel knew this was just as mortifying for the elderly woman as it was for him. Silently he handed her the change for a ten and bagged the book. He thanked her and said goodbye but she didn't make any eye contact and seemed to rush out of the shop.

"Is my lunch in the back room?" Summer asked when her customer had left. "Angel? Are you okay?"

His heart pounding in his chest, Angel looked down at the floor where the picture lay. Bending down to pick it up, he held onto it in a shaking hand.

Getting a glimpse of it, Summer rushed around the counter to stand along side of him to stare at it. "Holy shit!"

This time he didn't let her grab it out of his hand. Holding it far out of her reach, Angel gazed at it and hissed, "I don't believe this."

"What is that? Where did it come from? Angel, come on, let me see it."

Exhaling in defeat, Angel brought it closer so the two of them could inspect it. "It's a print-out from a computer. It's not an actual photograph," he muttered.

"How did it get here?" Summer asked, looking around the empty shop.

"I don't know. I suppose the same way the video got there. Someone is playing a sick joke on me."

"Ew, creepy." Summer shivered in exaggeration.

Eying the photo for a moment, Angel then spoke in a slow melancholy voice, "This shot was for one of the promos for another movie I did. I remember when it came out I got a phone call from my father. He was so enraged."

"Why? What did it have to do with him?"

Angel took a quick peek around the shop again, then continued, "My dad is a doctor. He has a lot of very well respected friends in the profession. When this photo showed up in the newspaper before the release of the film, he went berserk."

"They printed that photo?" She pointed to the obvious nudity.

"Well, not exactly, it had a black rectangle covering my genitals. The headline read, 'Loveday Has No Shame'. I remember it because it was a take off of the title of the film, *Shame*. My dad called me up, and he was so pissed off he ripped me a new one. He told me he was so embarrassed by it; he disowned me on the spot."

"Ouch."

"No kidding." Angel began crumbling it up in his hand as Summer tried to stop him. Growing annoyed, Angel pushed her hand away and crushed the paper into a ball.

"Stop hiding who you are!" Summer scolded.

"Oh? You want nude photos of you being slipped onto the counter while customers are here? Come on, Summer. Give me a break."

Though her expression was one of disappointment, she said, "Okay. I get it." When he tossed the paper into the trashcan behind the counter, she suggested, "Maybe you should call the police, Angel. I mean, if someone is leaving these things in the shop..."

"What are the police going to do?" Angel walked back to the office where their lunch waited.

"I don't know. Fingerprint the paper? Find out who's doing this to you?"

With Summer right behind him, Angel stood near his desk and handed her the paper sack containing her salad. "You eat first."

She took the bag, sitting down at his desk. "You sure you're okay?"

"I'm fine." He closed the door to give her privacy, then went to stand at the front counter again. Alone for the moment, he took the paper back out of the trash and unfolded it. Someone had printed this photo from the computer website that Oliver had found. All Angel wanted to know was why.

"Hey, Len," Oliver greeted him as Len approached him in the hallway of school.

"Hey, Oliver. You seen pimple-face yet today?"

Laughing at the joke, Oliver shook his head. "No. I think he cut class. I haven't seen him all day."

"What's with those songs he sings? It's like he's possessed." Len looked around the chaotic corridor.

"I know. But they're funny if you think about it. All that talk of Satan and shit."

"Funny? I think he's sick."

Oliver watched a group of students pass by, then replied, "Nah, he's okay. He's just trying to be different so we get noticed."

"Whatever." Len shrugged. "We getting together again to practice?"

"Yeah. My place. If you want to come after school, that's cool. Or next weekend. I don't care."

"Your dad's okay with all the noise?"

"Who cares?"

"We can go to my place tomorrow after school if you want."

"Okay. I just have to remember to bring my guitar." Oliver heard the bell ringing for class. "Gotta go!"

"Come by anyway, we can write some songs up that aren't demonic. See ya!" Len took off in the opposite direction.

Angel pulled into his driveway just as it started to rain. Climbing out of his car, he jogged to the front door of his home when he noticed something odd. As he drew nearer, he stopped short and looked around the front of his house to see if anyone was watching him. Before he touched anything, he used his key, opening the door, and shouted for Oliver. No sound returned. Sprinting through the house quickly, seeing it was empty, Angel hurried back to the front door and stared at the knife protruding from it.

"That's it. I've had enough." He picked up his cordless phone and dialed 911. "Yeah, hello. Look, my name is Gabriel Loveday, and I'd like to report something. Uh, what is it I'd like to report?" Angel stared at the knife. "I guess its property damage. Hell I don't know. Yes. Thank you." He gave her his name and address, hung up, and went to stand at the open door waiting for the police.

Twenty minutes later the rain had ceased. Angel watched as a patrol car pulled into his driveway. Two uniformed men stepped out and approached. Angel tried to keep his nerves calm. In the past his contacts with the police weren't always pleasant. This wasn't what he wanted to do, but he felt he had no choice. "Hello, gentlemen."

"Are you Mr. Loveday?" one of the cops asked, the younger of the two, taking out his pad from his chest pocket.

"Yes." Stepping aside, Angel pointed to the knife in his door stabbing through another naked print-out of him. "I came home about a half hour ago and found this."

As the two officers stared at it, Angel knew they were stifling a chuckle of amusement. One of them, the bigger, younger one who had asked him the first question did all the talking while the other older cop headed back to the patrol car for something.

"You have any idea who would do this?" the first cop asked.

"Not really."

"Where do you think they got that photo from?" He pointed to it with his pen.

"The net. I think someone downloaded it. Look, you can tell it's printed paper and not an actual photo."

"Don't touch it. We'll send it to the lab." The young cop looked over his shoulder to his partner. The second officer, now wearing rubber gloves, returned with two plain brown envelopes. The knife was extricated from the wood, placed into one envelope with the paper photo shoved into the other.

"Anything else happen lately that you think may be related?" the first cop asked.

"Yeah, uh, someone left one of my old videos on the counter of my bookshop in Redondo. Oh, and another one of those type of photos. A different one."

The second cop raised an eyebrow. "You have the other items?"

"No. My work colleague took the video home with her and I threw the photo out. Sorry."

The first cop asked, "What kind of old video? You mean a homemade movie?"

"Don't you know who this is?" the second cop asked the first. When his partner gave him a blank stare, the second cop said, "This is Angel Loveday. He was in all those Plimpton films."

Angel's face went beet red as the first cop gave him another good once over, saying, "Never heard of them."

"Good," Angel replied, his tone tinged with bitterness. "Anything else?"

"No. We'll send the two items to the lab. If anything comes of it, we'll let you know. Here's the case number." The first cop handed him a business card with a number handwritten on it. "If it happens again, use this number to refer to it, and we'll be able to connect all the different events."

Angel took the card, reading it. "Okay. Thanks for showing up."

"No problem."

Love You, Loveday

As the two officers walked back to their car, Angel overheard the younger one ask, "What the hell kind of movies was he in?"

"Soft porn," the older cop replied.

Angel cringed and closed the door.

By six o'clock Angel had his feet up on the coffee table, sipping a glass of wine. The front door opened and Oliver came in.

"Where the hell were you?" Angel asked.

"Out."

"You could have at least called."

"Yeah, whatever."

Hating Oliver's new cavalier attitude, Angel set his glass down on the low table and stood to confront him. "Oliver, don't walk away from me. I'm talking to you."

"Dad, leave me alone."

"Oliver Anthony Loveday! Get over here this minute before I get violent!"

At the severe tone, Oliver stopped and turned around.

Once Angel realized that Oliver was just going to stand there defiantly in reaction to the force of his voice, Angel was the one who closed the gap between them so they were nose to nose. "Why are you behaving this way?" Angel said, immediately getting a rolling of the eyes in response. "I'm not happy about it."

"What are you going to do? Throw me out like your old man did to you? Go ahead. I'll go make sex films on the internet."

Angel grabbed Oliver by his upper arms and lifted him off the ground. "Don't you dare talk to me that way."

"Put me down! Is this your 'respect' talk again? I'm supposed to respect some guy who gets his dick sucked for

35

money? You're no better than a stupid prostitute. Let go of me."

Angel shoved him back, causing Oliver to stumble to regain his balance. "Get away from me," Angel ordered. "I don't know what the hell's going on, Oliver, but I don't like it."

"Yeah? Too bad. I don't like you either."

The door slammed to Oliver's room, separating them. Angel knew this would happen if Oliver found out about his past. He knew it.

Chapter Five

Detective Billy Sharpe leafed through his in-box at the precinct in downtown Santa Monica. Loosening his tie and top collar button, he sat down at his desk with the pile of new cases and began reading. His coworker, Detective Jay Alexander, stopped by his desk, sipping a cup of coffee. "Anything good?"

Billy glanced up quickly from a report he was perusing. "Got one here from a guy who had a knife stuck in his door."

"Yeah? So what?"

"In Santa Monica? You know, one of those beach front properties."

"Oh? Are we getting as bad as LA? Why the hell would someone stick a knife into a door in that neighborhood?"

"I don't know."

"Any leads?"

Billy kept reading. "Patrol put two items into evidence, the knife and some photo of the victim."

"Sounds like harassment."

"Yeah, that's what I thought. They labeled it property damage."

"You want me to send it to the crimes against persons unit?"

Billy glanced up distractedly. "Hmm? No. I got it."

"You sure? If it ain't ours—"

"I said I got it."

"Suit yourself." Jay walked away.

When Jay had left, Billy stared at the name of the complainant/victim. *Gabriel Loveday*. He couldn't believe it. He'd had a hard-on for that man since he was eighteen. Whistling under his breath, he said, "Gabriel Angel Loveday... I can't fucking believe my luck." Reading the information on the report, Billy looked around the office to see how much privacy he would get before making a phone call, then called Angel's home number. No one answered. He tried the work number. "Yeah, hello, this is Detective Sharpe, I'm looking for Mr. Loveday."

"I'll get him for you, hang on," a woman said.

Billy tapped his pencil on the desk impatiently trying to imagine what this man looked like now.

"Hello? This is Angel, can I help you?"

"Mr. Loveday, this is Detective Sharpe. I was just looking over the report you filed yesterday."

"Oh. Okay."

Peering over the file cabinet to make sure Jay wasn't within hearing range, Billy spoke quietly, "I'd like to meet with you and have a chat about it."

"All right. I'm not sure what else I can say that I haven't already told the two officers that came by."

"Well, you never know. We may be able to brainstorm a little."

"You want to come here to the bookstore?"

"Bookstore?"

"Yes. It's where I work. In Redondo. My shop is called The Uncut Buzzard. There's a café next door where we can sit and have a cup of coffee."

"Oh. Great. Uh, I can be there in a few minutes."

"I'll be here."

Billy hung up and couldn't believe how excited he felt. Angel Loveday! Angel-fucking-Loveday! Oh, this was too good to be true.

"I'm glad you finally called the police, Angel." Summer added more horror fiction to the display.

"I'm not so sure it's going to do any good. They never find any of these idiots." Angel checked his watch nervously.

"You never know. They may get him on the fingerprints or something."

"Even if they do, come on, what difference does it make? You think I want to go to some court trial and have all my sordid past recounted in front of a jury, the press, and all of the damn world? No thanks."

"Well, you never know. They may just be able to give the guy a warning and at least he'll leave you alone."

When the door chime sounded they both spun around to look. Summer whispered, "Wow, who's that?"

Angel didn't know but he agreed with her appraisal.

"Gabriel Loveday?" the man in the business suit asked in a serious tone.

"Yes. Detective Sharpe?"

"Yes. Hello, Mr. Loveday."

"Call me Angel, please." Angel reached out to shake his extended hand.

"Angel," the detective said shyly.

"And this is my assistant, Summer Thompson." Angel gestured towards her.

As she shook the handsome detective's hand, she teased, "Hubba hubba! You can investigate me any day of the week."

"Behave yourself, young lady," Angel chided. "Forgive her, detective. She's just a kid."

"Hey!" Summer pretended to pout.

"We'll be next door if you need us. Okay, Summer?" Angel waited for her nod. He escorted the detective to the door. "This way, detective."

"Call me, Billy, please."

"Okay, Billy." Angel followed him out into the breezy ocean air. They walked the few paces to the café and Billy opened the door for them. As they stood at the counter together Angel asked, "What would you like, Billy?"

"Coffee, please, Angel."

Angel shouted to Mary, "Two coffees, Mary, please?"

"Right away, Angel!" She waved to him.

"Have a seat, Billy." Angel directed him to a small table and waited as the detective sat down, opening his jacket button. "Mary will bring them over to us."

"All right."

Sitting across from him, Angel estimated this handsome man to be close to his own age. Fantastically fit, a full head of dark black hair and brilliant blue eyes. Angel didn't want to salivate over him, but it was getting hard to prevent. As Billy's jacket parted and the shoulder holster emerged, creating a powerful image, Angel almost creamed his jeans at the excitement he was feeling. When the hell was the last time he got a hard-on from just looking at a man? 1985?

Billy took a pad and pen from out of his jacket pocket, appearing all business for the moment. Right before he began asking Angel questions, Mary brought over their coffees, setting out sugar and cream for them.

"Thanks, sweetheart." Angel winked at her.

"My pleasure, dear."

After she left, Angel stirred some milk into his cup. "Fire away," he smiled.

"Right." Billy read over his notes. "When did all of this

start? Is it recent?"

"Yes, very recent. Last Friday was the first time. Someone left my film *Filth* on the counter of the shop."

"Left it and ran? Did you see anyone?"

"No. It was before we opened. Summer came here to get us a coffee and I was in the office. We didn't have the door locked. I heard the door chime. Twice, actually. I heard it twice. I thought it was Summer coming back, but it wasn't. Someone obviously just hurried in, left it on the counter, and took off."

Billy nodded, writing notes. But all the while he was remembering that movie. Oh, yes, the first of the Plimpton/Loveday partnership. The debut of one of the most fantastic gay icons in American history. Who didn't know his name back then? Have a poster of him on their wall? Thumb hungrily through the naughty magazines for a glimpse of his cock? That famous, enormous Loveday cock. *And look at him now*. Billy did a discreet once over of this incredible man's face, his long straight hair, and tight muscular upper body. Still gorgeous. Absolutely gorgeous.

Billy crossed his legs under the table as his cock throbbed. "Right. So, what do you think? A crazed fan?"

"Christ. I hope not. I had enough of that in the Eighties. I swear I had no peace."

"I can imagine. You were one heck of a sex symbol back then."

Angel stopped mid sip, staring at him.

At the intensity of Angel's gaze, Billy sensed a faux pas. His face went crimson. Lifting his cup to his mouth, Billy tried to hide behind it.

"You know my movies?" Angel asked in surprise.

"Yeah. Of course."

"How old are you? If you don't mind me asking."

"No, I don't mind. Thirty-nine." Billy wondered what Angel was thinking. His expression was unreadable.

"You're in damn good shape for thirty-nine."

Billy's face blushed deeply at the compliment from a man he idolized, he replied, "Ditto."

"Thank you, detective." Angel smiled sweetly. "Ah, any other questions?"

Feeling carried away at the moment by their flirty banter, Billy blurted out, "Yeah, you want to get dinner later?" then felt like a complete idiot.

To Billy's astonishment, Angel grinned wickedly and replied, "Yes."

"Wow. Great." Billy cleared his throat and set his cup down, missing the saucer and awkwardly causing a clatter.

Leaning closer to Billy from across the table, Angel asked, "So, you liked my movies?"

"Fucking loved them."

"I can't tell you how flattered I am."

"Good. Very good." Trying to get under control, Billy rubbed his own cock discreetly under the table as it began aching from the excitement.

Angel caught the gesture. *Maybe something good will come out of this horrible mess.* "I have to admit, Billy, I don't usually like to discuss my past with anyone. I feel embarrassed to have done those films. I sometimes wish I hadn't done them, or that they would vanish off the planet and I didn't have to hear about them anymore."

"No way." Billy shook his head. "That's absurd."

"I'm serious. I've gotten so much flack for them. You know my parents disowned me?" Angel noticed the detective shifting in his chair again. *Dealing with a hard-on?* Angel wondered.

"That's unfair. I really think they were out of line, Angel. Look, maybe some of those pseudo-religious-Bible-thumpers thought they were obscene, but you had one hell of a fan club, gorgeous."

Blinking his eyes in shock, Angel echoed, "Gorgeous?"

When it appeared Billy was mortified by his own comment, Angel tried to comfort him. "Hey, don't look so petrified. I'm loving every minute of this."

"Thank fuck. I didn't want you to complain to my lieutenant that I was sexually harassing you."

"Don't worry. It's a welcome advance for a change." Angel wanted to touch him. The animal magnetism of this police detective was irresistible.

"I can't believe you're coming to dinner with me."

"Why?" Angel finished his coffee.

"I don't know. I mean, I assumed you would be taken. How can a man like you be available?"

A nasty feeling washed over Angel's body. *Oliver, that's why.*

It was obvious Billy read the change of his countenance because he asked, "What's wrong? Did I finally stuff my foot in my mouth?"

"No. No, Billy, you didn't. If you want to know the truth, I've been avoiding having a relationship with a man because of my son, Oliver. But, lately, he's been so different, so distant, I don't know what to do for the best anymore."

"You have a son?"

"Yes. I was married for a short time. My wife died of cancer when Oliver was seven. He's sixteen now. I've been trying to shield him from my past and all the shit I've done, and the fact that I am gay."

"Your son doesn't know you're gay?" Billy leaned his elbows on the small table, speaking quietly.

"He does now. He's finally found all my old movies and photos on the internet. I was sickened when he did. But I suppose it was unrealistic to believe he would never find out. Someone obviously told him."

"And when did all this happen?"

"Why? You think there's some kind of correlation between him knowing and the incidences?"

"Could be."

"No. Oliver would never do that. He's a good boy, Billy. He's not the type."

"All right. I'll take your word for it. So, where am I taking you to dinner tonight, Angel?"

Feeling his heart melt at that lovely smile, Angel reached over the table to touch Billy's hand and replied, "Anywhere you desire."

When Angel returned to the bookshop he found Summer near the nonfiction shelf busy assisting a customer. Trying not to distract her, he stood behind the counter in case someone needed help. Angel looked forward to meeting Billy later on for a nice dinner of seafood at the Redondo Pier.

The gentleman Summer had been helping brought his book to the cash register to purchase. Angel rung it up for him and watched him leave, then waited as Summer leaned over the counter for a chat.

"So? Will they find the guy who did this to you?"

"I don't know."

"Maybe they will, Angel. You have to keep an open mind."

Smiling, wanting to tell her he had a date with the detective, he decided not to mention it in case it made Summer jealous in any way. "I will, Summer. I will."

When four o'clock arrived, Angel called home from the phone in his office to let Oliver know he was going out for dinner. No one answered and the machine picked up. About to hang up in irritation, Angel instead left Oliver a message, "Hey, babe, it's me. I'm going out with a friend for dinner at the pier, so you're on your own for a meal. There's some frozen stuff in the freezer you can microwave if you want. I shouldn't be home late. See ya later." He hung up and felt nervous that suddenly Oliver wasn't coming straight home after school when previously they'd spent every night together sharing their daily events as they ate dinner. The change in Oliver was so drastic, Angel began to suspect drugs may be a part of the problem and hoped he was wrong.

Summer popped her head into the office. "We ready to lock up, boss?"

"We are." Angel made sure the safe was closed and secured, following Summer out to the front door. He set the alarm, then they stood outside and locked the shop up tight.

"See ya tomorrow, Angel." Summer waved.

"Goodnight, Summer." Angel waved back and then began the short stroll down to the pier and the restaurant. The wind was picking up and the warmth of the day had left, replaced by cool autumn air coming off the ocean. Twilight approached and very few people were out strolling on the beach. The shops were closing for the night.

Litter and sand blew in rippling waves over the paved sidewalk. A piece of paper danced in front of him. Just about to step around it, Angel paused, then reached down to pick it up. As it unfurled in the wind, he groaned, "Oh, no, you have to be kidding me." Yet another naked photograph of him printed off a computer was literally floating around in public. But on this one, a title had been added. "Prince of Porn". Just as Angel started to crumble it up in his hands, he noticed another. Slowly he approached it, his heart beating so fast he felt it in his throat.

There, nailed to the tree like a crucifixion was his image;

his arms spread wide as if reaching to the ends of the page, his pelvis thrust forward, and the classic Loveday seductive expression on his face. Or as Plimpton used to call it, the "come fuck me" look. In red marker across the top, "Prince of Porn" blazed like a tattoo in blood.

Angel ripped it down, looking back in the direction from where he'd come and noticed on each tree that lined the street, paper flapped in the stiff breeze. Jogging back to the next tree, he found the same photo hung there. The feeling of ice in his veins made him dizzy. From tree to tree, all the way back to his shop, he removed the pictures, which hung like posters for an upcoming event. Seeing that none of the photos extended beyond the bookshop, Angel checked the time, knew he was now running late, and had a pile of the pictures collected in his fist. About to toss them out in the nearest trashcan, he decided to show them to Billy, since they were meeting shortly, and it did seem logical to tell the police now that one report was filed.

Keeping a tight grip on the wad of paper in his hand, Angel continued his walk, pulling down the few that remained as he headed northbound to the restaurant.

Billy checked his watch again. He was standing in front of the restaurant entrance, wondering if Angel had a case of cold feet. He didn't have a cell phone number for Angel but decided to give him the benefit of the doubt and wait another ten minutes. Finally, emerging from out of the dusky gloom, Billy spotted Angel coming towards him. A feeling of relief washed over him, until he read Angel's infuriated expression, then that relief changed to worry. Hurrying to meet him, Billy said, "I had no idea you had to walk. I would have picked you up. Are you all right? Did something happen?"

Without a word, Angel showed him the pile of crushed paper in his hand. Immediately Billy touched Angel's arm and brought him out of the mainstream of foot traffic to the side of a retaining wall so they could have some shelter from the wind.

Billy took the papers Angel had been clinging to and inspected them. "Where the hell were they?"

"I found them on every fucking tree from my shop to the end of the walkway."

Billy gave a quick count, "Twenty?"

"I don't know."

Seeing how upset he was, he led Angel to his unmarked police car. Billy opened the passenger door for him, allowing Angel to sit down, then went to the driver's side and climbed in next to him. In the relative privacy of the car's interior, Billy flipped on the dome light to get a better look at the photos. Instantly he recognized the familiar Loveday pose, then read the handwritten title. "Christ." He shook his head. "The asshole means to torment you. I think you have yourself a stalker, Angel." Waiting for a reply, Billy tilted his head to look at Angel and found him rubbing his face in anguish. Billy set photos on the floor, face down, in the back seat, then reached out to comfort Angel, rubbing his arm warmly. "Let me buy you a drink."

"Why the fuck is this happening?" Angel groaned. "What did I do? I didn't do anything to anyone. I'm just minding my own fucking business."

"You did nothing. Stop blaming yourself. You know how many nut-cases there are out there?" Billy gestured to outside the car. "I'm afraid celebrities get targeted all the time, Angel. It's nothing new."

"I'm not a fucking celebrity."

Oh, like hell you're not. Billy said, "It happens all the time." Patting Angel's thigh, he asked, "You want to pass on dinner? You want me to drive you home?"

"No. No, I'm all right. Let's grab a bite."

"Okay...hang on," Billy replied, then had a good look around the car and the immediate area. When the coast was clear, he reached behind Angel's amazing head of long hair and drew him close. Without the slightest hesitation, that incredible star of the Plimpton films kissed him. On contact Billy knew damn well he could get carried away it was so enticing. After exploring Angel's tongue and mouth gently, Billy sat back and smiled at him.

Angel grinned shyly back. "Wow."

"Feeling better?" Billy wanted to screw him right there, right then.

"Oh, yes...I feel like a million bucks." Angel laughed softly.

"It's what you're worth, gorgeous, believe me. Come on. Dinner. My treat."

The kiss worked magic. Angel felt infinitely better. They climbed out of the dark sedan and walked side by side into the restaurant. The hostess showed them a table overlooking the choppy seawater. In the dim light, the single candle in the middle of the table created a seductive aura that could lure enemies to reunite. Angel loved the ambiance and was swept up in the romance, imagining he and this handsome detective were already a committed couple. They sat down and took the menus they were handed. Once the hostess left, Angel set the menu down and smiled adoringly at Billy. "So, tell me about yourself. I don't know a damn thing."

Laying his menu down, as well, Billy opened the button of his suit jacket to get comfortable. "What do you want to know?"

"Ever married? Any kids?" Angel moved his legs so that his and Billy's were touching each other under the table.

"Never married, no kids."

"Are you out?"

"No. Not at work anyway. A few of my closest friends know, but that's it. As far as I'm concerned, it's nobody's fucking business."

Angel loved the sound of his voice. It had a slight accent to it. East Coast? Whatever it was, it made Billy sound confident, masculine, and sexy.

"I understand," Angel replied. "Believe me. I didn't even want my son Oliver to know."

They were interrupted by the waiter asking them for their drink order. Billy requested a beer, Angel a glass of red wine. When the man left them, Billy continued their conversation. "Yeah, about your kid. He acting up?"

Angel's calm expression changed. "Yes. I don't know what the hell's wrong with him. It's hard for me to believe this is all down to my film history, but I know it is."

"Come on. He's sixteen, right? He's not a baby. He can understand you had a different life back then. There's no reason for him to go nuts."

"I'm not so sure." Angel nodded for Billy to stop talking as the waiter set their drinks down.

"You ready to order?" the waiter asked.

"No, give us another minute," Billy responded. The waiter nodded and left.

Once they were alone again, Angel sipped his wine and asked, "You ever been in a serious relationship?"

"Yeah, once. It lasted about five years. He ended up cheating on me, so we split up."

"How long ago was that?"

"A year."

"Oh? That recent?"

Billy picked up the menu that had rested under his elbows. "It ain't recent. I haven't been laid in a damn year." When he met Angel's eyes, Billy bit his lip. "I didn't mean it like you were just here for a fuck. Sorry it came out that way."

Angel laughed. "I love your directness. Christ, it's so refreshing."

"Yeah? Most people think I'm an arrogant ass." Billy

flipped open the menu.

"Yeah?" Angel mimicked him. "Most people think I'm a porn star. Welcome to the world of perceptions and misconceptions."

"Screw everyone. I don't give a shit."

Angel leaned over the table to whisper, "You always wear a gun?"

The change in topics appeared to surprise Billy. "Why? You okay with it?"

"Yes. I'm fine with it. It makes you look fucking sexy."

"Really?" Billy smiled, sitting up in the chair. "No one ever told me that before."

"I'll bet you have women swooning over you." Angel winked at him.

"I don't give a rat's ass about women."

"What do you 'give a rat's ass' about, detective?" Angel purred seductively.

Lowering the menu so they could see each other more clearly, Billy whispered, "About getting my hands on you, you gorgeous mother fucker. Now stop cock-teasing me so I can order, will ya?"

Angel burst out laughing and took another sip of his wine. He was on fire. He couldn't take his eyes off of Billy, and he couldn't wait to see him naked.

Oliver called out for his father as he came through the door. "He's not here," he said as he entered the living room with Perry. "You want something to drink?" Oliver asked, setting his backpack down on the floor near the couch.

"Nah. When do you think your dad will be back?"

"Don't know." Oliver checked the phone messages and hit the button when he found it flashing. The sound of his father's voice came out of the machine.

Oliver and Perry exchanged looks. Oliver said, "He's out."

"You know which friend he's with?" Perry followed Oliver into the kitchen.

"No. Who cares?" Oliver opened the refrigerator and took out a bottle of cola.

"Is it a guy? Is he out with a guy?" Perry asked.

"Shut up, Perry. Why do you ask me so many questions about my dad?" Oliver poured the soda into a glass.

"I just think he's cool, that's all. He's got a really big dick."

Oliver cringed. "You keep talking about him like that and you can just get lost."

Perry left the kitchen.

Shaking his head, Oliver sipped his drink, then set it on the table so he could search the freezer for a meal. After he stuck something into the microwave, he looked for Perry. Oliver found him sitting in front of the computer in his bedroom. Standing behind Perry, Oliver looked at the sites he was bringing up. "Man, you never stop." Oliver shook his head.

"Have you seen this one?" Perry leaned to one side so Oliver had a better view. "That guy there, the one he's sucking? He died of AIDS in 1990."

"Ew, shut up. Why the hell are you telling me that?"

"That guy was a real porno star. He did some really dirty movies. Much worse than your dad did."

"Look, Per, I'm tired. You mind just going now? I'll see you tomorrow after school or something. Okay?"

"Yeah, okay." Perry pushed out the chair and stood.

The moment he moved away from the computer, Oliver shut it down, sickened by the images on the screen.

"Are we getting together this Saturday to practice in your garage?" Perry asked as he headed to the front door.

"I suppose. My dad's got some Halloween party coming

up. But I don't know which weekend it is. I guess it doesn't matter if he's here or not anyway."

"A Halloween party? Where?"

"The woman he works with is having it. Dad wanted me to go with him, but I think hanging around a bunch of drunk old people sounds like a drag."

"The woman he works with? That blonde lady?"

"Yeah. Summer. She lives somewhere in Wilmington."

"Huh."

"Huh, what?" Oliver heard the bell on the microwave chime letting him know his dinner was ready.

"Nothing. Just that I love Halloween parties."

"Really?"

"Yeah, if it was me, I'd go."

Oliver narrowed his eyes at Perry. "You would not. Shut up."

"I would. If you tell me when and where that party is, I'll go with you."

"Oh." Oliver considered it. "Let me ask my dad—"

"No! Don't tell him I want to go. He'll think I'm a dork. Don't mention it."

"Man, you really are weird, Perry. Anyway, my dinner is done. Let me eat it. I'm starved." He walked Perry to the door. "See ya."

"See ya, Oliver."

Heading back to the kitchen to eat, Oliver wondered if going to Summer's party would be more fun with his friend there.

After the meal, Angel walked with Billy to the parking lot.

"Let me give you a lift back to your car." Billy unlocked the car doors with an electronic key fob.

"Thanks." Angel climbed into the passenger seat after a quick peek into the back to see the pile of papers still stacked on the floor.

"I'll turn those into evidence tomorrow morning," Billy said, obviously noticing Angel had glanced at them.

Nodding, trying not to let it invade his good mood, Angel fastened his seatbelt as Billy started the car and drove him back to the bookshop's parking lot. Daydreaming, trying not to think about what nasty surprises the future held with this unknown "stalker", Angel returned to the present as they pulled up next to his Camaro, the only car left in the lot.

Billy placed his car in park and turned, facing Angel, his arm on the seat behind him.

When Angel felt Billy's hand caressing his hair gently, he leaned towards it, asking for more. Instantly, Billy went for his lips, urging Angel forward for a kiss. Connecting to Billy's hungry mouth made Angel's skin light on fire. He cupped Billy's rough jaw and lapped lusciously at his lips and tongue, savoring the taste of a man he was incredibly attracted to. Billy's left hand cupped Angel's crotch. The heat of Billy's palm made Angel open his legs wider for him.

At one point in their kissing, Billy pulled back to pant for air. "Christ, I'm so fucking horny. Where could we go? You want to go somewhere?"

Angel smiled lazily, replying, "I'd love to, but I have to see if Oliver is all right."

Billy checked his watch. "It's early. You want to call him?"

"I don't have a cell phone."

Billy took his out of his pocket. "Here. See if he's okay."

"You sure?" Angel took the tiny phone.

"Of course."

Flipping it open, Angel dialed his home number as Billy wrapped his fingers softly around Angel's long locks. "Oliver?

It's me. Did you get my message?"

"Yeah."

"You eat dinner?"

"Yeah."

Angel hated this game Oliver was playing, hated it. "You okay? You need me to come home?"

"I'm fine. No, I don't need you. Are you out with a guy?"

Angel glanced at Billy's concerned expression. "Uh, no. I'm out with Summer. We were thinking of catching a late movie. I just wanted to make sure that was okay with you first."

"I don't care."

"You have homework to do?"

"Daaaad!"

"All right, I'm just asking. I'll be home by around ten. Okay?"

"Yeah. See ya."

When he hung up, Angel looked at the tiny digital display and hit the disconnect button. Handing it to Billy, his son's apathetic words rebounding in his head, Angel didn't know what to do any longer and began to feel sick about it.

After Billy took back the phone and slipped it into his pocket, he kissed Angel's cheek and whispered, "My place?"

A wave of guilt washed over Angel. Lying to his son, knowing the gulf between them was growing, wishing he could somehow repair the damage; all this crap spun in his head while the handsome man next to him lured him into his bed.

Billy wanted him so badly he would go mad if Angel said no. Trying not to push him, sitting back so Angel could decide freely, Billy kept staring at Angel's long, tight denim-covered thighs and bulging crotch. They were the only things well lit from the outside streetlights. Angel's upper body was in shadow. But those legs kept Billy enthralled. Finding them irresistible, He smoothed his hand from Angel's hip to his knee, and back again, savoring the solid muscle underneath. When Angel kept still as if he were trying to be persuaded, Billy leaned closer to kiss Angel's neck, run tiny kisses up to his ear, chewing on his earlobe. A sound of longing emerged from Angel's throat. Hearing it, Billy went for that hot crotch again, cupping his palm over it and getting a sense of its size. "You're driving me insane," he confided, "my cock is going to explode."

Angel began laughing. "Okay, detective. I'll follow you."

"Great. Don't change your mind, baby. Please."

"I won't." Angel kissed his lips, then climbed out of the car, walking to his Camaro.

Billy shifted his body to sit correctly in the driver's seat, waiting for Angel to start his car. When Angel's headlights came on, Billy led the way to his home in Inglewood, all the while keeping his eyes on his rearview mirror hoping Angel wouldn't reconsider.

Angel parked in the driveway behind Billy's unmarked patrol car. A pleasant looking split-level home with finely trimmed landscaping came into view in the dim streetlight as he stepped outside his car. Pocketing his keys, Angel met him at the front door, where Billy opened the lock, then disarmed a security alarm. They stepped into the living room together and Angel waited as Billy shut the door behind them.

"You want anything? Something to drink?" Billy offered, taking off his suit jacket.

When Angel caught sight of the brown leather holster and handgun, he closed the gap between them quickly. Running his palm over the smooth leather at Billy's shoulder, Angel whispered, "I want you."

As if it was what Billy had been waiting to hear, he wrapped around Angel's waist and embraced him, kissing him passionately and swaying as their hips locked together. Only making out for a brief moment, Billy parted from their kiss, then held Angel's hand and led him to the bedroom. He turned on a dim light that sat on a nightstand and began taking off his shoulder holster. Before he did, Angel moved closer, helping Billy open the leather buckle to slide it off. Once it was loose, Billy took the holster with the gun and placed it down on his dresser, then he crossed the carpeted floor once again to help Angel remove his shirt.

When Angel felt the cool air rush across the skin of his back and chest, he checked Billy's expression to see if he was pleased with what he saw. And as if Billy could read Angel's mind, he crooned, "Christ, you are fantastic."

Angel smiled in relief as Billy leaned down to take his right nipple into his mouth. Feeling Billy's teeth nipping it until it was hard, Angel began shifting his weight in anticipation of things to come. Cupping Billy's head, Angel enjoyed the tongue-nipple teasing immensely. When Billy stood up straight once again, he had the look of someone who has found nirvana. Feeling like the play-toy for this powerful police officer, Angel waited submissively so he could do whatever Billy wanted him to do.

Billy didn't know where to start. It was as if he had a buffet of delicacies, all his favorites, and he had all night to devour them. Though he was still fully clothed, he had to get Angel naked. Memories of those films, this erotic actor standing nude while the rest of the cast was covered up, his face fiercely proud, his body perfection, and his modesty unheard of; Billy reached down for that button and zipper, his hands began to shake he was so excited. As Angel waited, patient as a saint, Billy spread wide the light blue faded denim and got his first glimpse of that flat washboard abdomen and pelvis. It was all he needed to go completely mad. With a hand on each end of Angel's waistband, Billy yanked those skin-tight jeans down to the floor. After he had, finding nothing underneath, he sat back and got his first look at Angel Loveday in the flesh, not the soft-porn movie actor on screen. This was reality.

And it was worth everything he owned. How many times did he jerk off to that image? How many nights did he dream of touching this man? This matinee idol, this fantasy? Too many.

As Angel stood exposed in the cool, dim room, he knew exactly what Billy was thinking as he gaped at him. Or did he? How many people had begged Angel for a fuck? How many men and women offered themselves to him? Too many. There was one thing Angel yearned for, love, commitment, not a casual screw.

"Billy?" he whispered, once the pause became too long. When he noticed Billy dabbing at his eyes, Angel grew concerned and knelt down to be at the same level as Billy was. "What's wrong?"

Then as if it were almost impossible to speak, Billy managed to say slowly, "You know how long I have loved you?"

A dam burst inside Angel. He wrapped around this kind man and hugged him tight. "Oh, baby, you have me now. You have me now."

Billy fell back with Angel onto the soft pile carpet, rolling around the floor with him, kissing his lips, rubbing his hands all over Angel's skin. As those hot masculine hands fondled him, Angel's head spun in delight. How long had it been? Decades. Almost two decades of no contact, terrified Oliver would find out, frightened of being used and left. Not now. Not by this man. No way. Angel knew he was a good judge of character. His life had depended on it at times. And he knew this man was a good man. Honest, wholesome, and incredibly hot.

Straddling Angel's hips, Billy sat up and started pulling off his tie, his button-down shirt, throwing them onto the floor. With his hands still trembling at the possibility of being able to screw his beloved icon, he opened the zipper of his dress slacks, then knelt up to get them off, yearning for skin on skin, cock on cock.

Once he was naked, he stood up, reaching his hand down to help Angel to his feet and onto the bed. Watching Angel spread out naked on the mattress, Billy had to close his eyes to control himself. It had to be a dream. This couldn't be reality.

"Come get it, babe," Angel whispered. "You've waited long enough."

Feeling emotional and cursing himself for it, Billy rubbed his face, trying to get under control before he turned into an animal and devoured this sex god.

And as if Angel knew what Billy was going through, even possibly experienced it before, he reached out, dragging Billy on top.

Just the scent of Angel drove him crazy. Billy sniffed at his skin, his hair, his neck, rubbing his hips against Angel's trying to get friction, get inside, get anywhere and come.

Again Angel attempted to get them back on track as Billy lost himself on Angel's body. "Do you have a rubber, babe? And some lube?" Angel asked gently.

"Yes. Yes... Here." Billy sat up and reached into the top drawer of his nightstand. He dropped a condom onto the bed next to Angel, then showed him a tube of lubrication.

"Good," Angel hissed. "Very good."

As Billy knelt up and watched, Angel put a condom on him. Just the touch of Angel's hands on his cock was maddening him to new heights. When Angel rolled over and offered his ass, Billy thought he would pass out. Not wasting a chance of a lifetime, Billy hurried to move behind Angel, holding those narrow hips of his. "You okay?" Billy asked.

"Yes, you don't worry about it. You just get in there and play. Okay?"

Awash with chills at his amazing words, Billy knelt up and

placed the tip of his dick against Angel's ass. Inhaling a deep breath, knowing he would come the moment he penetrated, Billy pushed in and shivered from his scalp to his toes. As if unable to prevent it, Billy's body went into overdrive. Pumping in deliciously, hearing Angel's moans of pleasure and encouragement, Billy's body went into a spasm of ecstasy and shot come out so hard he thought he would explode. Taking a long moment to savor the heat and depth of Angel's body, Billy finally pulled out, sitting back on his heels to recuperate. Once he did, Angel rolled over to smile at him. "Good one?"

"Oh, my fucking god."

"Good!" Angel chuckled.

Coming back to life, Billy tossed the spent rubber on the floor, then dove down on Angel, stuffing that world famous large cock into his mouth. Giving the best head he could possibly give, Billy knew that Angel had his cocked sucked so many times, it would be impossible to compete. But he tried. He wanted it to be a memorable one. As Billy worked him, he almost forgot Angel's pleasure, as his own was riding high once more. Peeking up at Angel's incredible face as he climbed into orgasmic pleasure, Billy felt his own body reacting. He knew he wouldn't be able to get enough of Angel. It was too much of his boyhood fantasies to ever get enough.

Thrusting Angel's long cock into his throat, lapping at it hungrily, grabbing it tightly around the base, handling those soft, heavy balls, it was a dream, yet he was awake, not dreaming. When that hard organ rippled and Billy tasted the salty drop on his tongue, he sucked harder, faster, more wildly until Angel arched his back and came, grunting loudly and gripping the sheets under him.

Billy closed his eyes in pleasure and swallowed down Angel's sperm like it was honey. As Angel recovered, Billy licked him gently, lovingly. Sensing Angel's breathing and pulse slowing back to normal, Billy crawled up on the bed to lie beside him, cradling him in his arms. "Thank you. Oh, Angel, thank you."

"My pleasure, Billy, believe me. It was my pleasure."

Angel knew he didn't have all night to savor the cuddles and afterglow. As they lay intertwined under a light blanket, Angel felt his eyes grow heavy and knew he should leave before he fell asleep. He just didn't want to.

"You have to go?" Billy asked, checking the time.

"I do."

"I understand. Look, we'll get together again soon. Let's not get too melodramatic about it. We have plenty of time ahead of us to play with each other. Am I right?"

Angel rolled over to smile at Billy as he rested against the pillows. "You're right. Okay. Let me get dressed then."

After a kiss, Angel climbed out of the bed with Billy following after. They both got dressed quickly, in jeans.

As Billy tucked in his t-shirt he escorted Angel to the front door. "Oh, I meant to ask you. How did you get the name Angel? Is that some stage name?"

"It's a nickname, actually." Angel took his car keys out of his pocket. "My first name is Gabriel. So my mother thought that was too angelic to ignore. She called me Angel since I was a young kid."

"I get it. I like it. I can't imagine you as a Gabe, or a Gabriel. Angel fits."

"I thought so, too." He paused to smile at Billy. "See ya soon?"

"Oh. Look, if anything else funny happens, don't call 911. You call me. You understand?" Billy took out a business card from his wallet. "This has my cell phone number on it. No matter what time something happens, you ring me and I'll be there in a flash. You got it?"

"You sure? What if you're at work?" Angel fingered the

card.

"You call me." Billy pointed a warning finger at him. "No exceptions."

"Okay, I will, babe. Maybe my 'admirer' has gone away."

"I doubt it. You're not an easy man to get out of the blood, Loveday."

Angel smiled sweetly. "You say all the right things, don't you, detective?"

"I try. You just watch your ass. It means a hell of a lot to me."

"I will. I'll be okay. See ya soon."

"I'll call ya tomorrow. At work, okay?"

"Yeah, anytime." Angel kissed him, then left. When he looked back, Billy was watching as he got into his car. He waved at him, very happy to have that man as his guardian angel.

Angel came through the door just after ten. He peeked into Oliver's bedroom and found him fast asleep. Sighing with relief, he headed to the shower to wash up and then went to bed.

Chapter Six

The next morning, Oliver left for the bus stop still giving Angel the silent treatment. Throwing up his hands in frustration, Angel was tired of one-way conversations, which inevitably turned into a one-way shouting match. Ending with, "I'm warning you, Oliver! Stop being my damn judge and jury. I had enough of that twenty years ago."

Oliver slammed the front door.

In the calm that followed, Angel rubbed his weary face and knew telling Oliver he had a new boyfriend most likely wasn't a very good idea at the moment.

Grabbing his keys and locking up his home, Angel drove to the shop, checking his watch and wishing he wasn't eternally rushing. It seemed as if things weren't as under control as they usually were, and he disliked the sensation of a nervous stomach. Where was he a week ago? He and his son were best friends, and he had felt very confident and normal. Now? Sick to his stomach and not even on speaking terms with Oliver. What the hell was going on?

Parking next to Summer's Mazda in the lot, Angel hurried around the front of the building to open the shop. Summer was there waiting, leaning back against the window.

"I have to remember to get you a key," Angel said the moment he spotted her. "Please, remind me. This has gone on too long, and I have no idea why you don't have one. You're always here before me and waiting." He opened the door and put the code into the alarm box.

"It's no problem, Angel. Don't worry about it. I'm chronically early. But you do have something else to worry about."

He stopped short and spun around to face her. Rarely did Summer use a serious tone. "What now?"

"This." She held out a flier.

He assumed it was part of the collection he had ripped down the night before. "Oh. Another one? Great," he said bitterly. "Where did you find this one?" He took it from her and then exclaimed, "Wait a minute…this one's different."

"Different? Different than what?" Summer leaned against Angel's side to look at the photo again.

"Crap," Angel mumbled. "I found around twenty pictures like this last night. They were nailed to the trees all along the sidewalk almost to the end of the shopping area. But it wasn't this photograph. It was a different one. Jesus! Why won't this idiot leave me alone?"

"What's the deal with the caption? I don't like it, Angel, it's too scary."

Angel read the words "Love you Loveday," that were written in the same blood red color as the last one. "The other picture said 'Prince of Porn'. Nice, huh?"

"You should call the cops. They need to see that one. Oop! I touched it. We both did. Does that mean they can't fingerprint it anymore?"

"I don't know." Angel brooded as he walked to the back office. As he did, Summer yelled, "I'll get the lattes!"

He didn't answer and forgot to give her petty cash. Instead he sat down at his desk, set the photo down on it and stared at it. The memories it was evoking were more powerful than ever. That day, the day this photo was taken he had just turned nineteen.

"Angel-baby…don't look so funereal. It's our biggest movie yet. Come on, baby-doll, give me that seductive smile for the camera."

"Shut up, Buster," Angel grumbled at his director. "Why naked? Why do I always have to be naked?"

"Angel-doll-face…because you are the star…the Greek god of legend. And what have you got to be ashamed of? Huh? Look at you? You're perfect, baby, perfect. Now, where's that Loveday charm? Huh? Smile for the camera, baby. Give William your best Loveday sex appeal."

Angel raised his chin in defiance, threw down the small towel he was using to cover himself, then faced the fan blowing back his hair. The moment he felt in control, he tilted his head seductively and grinned, that demonic, fuck-me grin that Buster Plimpton wanted so badly.

"Perfect, Angel! Perfect, baby! Oh, we're gonna be rich on this one. Rich."

"Well, Buster was right about one thing. We both got rich," Angel mused out loud. Picking up his phone from the desk, Angel dialed a number he committed to memory the moment he read it. "Hello? Billy? It's me."

"Hello, gorgeous. I've been thinking of you all morning. You enjoy last night?"

At the sound of his voice, Angel immediately felt better. "I did. You're an amazing man, Detective Sharpe."

"And you say I say all the right things."

Angel laughed softly.

"So, when can I see you again? You free tonight?" Billy asked.

"Yes and no. I need to get home. I think being away from the house is making Oliver even more distant. But why don't you come by."

"You sure? You want me there with the kid? You think that's a good idea? Did you even tell him about us?"

"No. I chickened out. I can say you're just a friend. Can't I?"

"Up to you, Angel. I defer to your judgment."

"Let me think about it. Either way, I will see you, even if it's just for a few hours."

"Okay. No problem."

"Oh…" Angel looked down at the picture. "I don't want to bother you about this but…"

"What happened?"

"Another photo showed up this morning. My coworker, Summer, found it and gave it to me when I arrived. I have it here. We both touched it though, so I don't know if you'll be able to get prints."

"I'll come by and get it. I'm also going to call the lab and see if there was anything back on either the knife or paperwork we already submitted."

"Okay." Angel set the paper aside on his desk just as Summer returned with the coffees. Cupping the phone he said to her, "Take some money out of the petty cash box."

She nodded, setting the coffees down and locating the little metal box.

Billy asked, "You got someone there?"

"Yes, Summer is here."

"Okay, I'll let you go. I'll come by in about an hour. Or better yet, can I take you to lunch?"

"Summer and I usually eat here. With just the two of us working, it's better if we're not on our own completely."

"I understand. No problem."

"But you can join me for a bite here, in the back office."

Laughing at the suggestion, Billy said, "I'll let you know. All right, Angel. See ya in a few."

"Bye, Billy." When he hung up Summer was smiling at him.

"Billy?" she asked. "Who's Billy?"

"Yeah…uh, you remember the detective—"

"No!" she choked. "You mean that handsome police officer is gay?"

"Yes. Did I luck out or what?" Angel sipped his coffee. "You lock the front door?"

"No. Should I?"

"Yes, please. While this idiot is around stalking me, we shouldn't let the shop go unattended."

Placing her coffee down on the desk, Summer gasped, "Did you say stalking?"

"Go lock the door."

She nodded and rushed out. While she was gone, Angel sipped his cup, staring at the picture. He heard her say, "Uh oh." Jolting out of his chair, he rushed out of the office to the shop. She was standing at the counter, staring down at it. With his heart once again beating madly, he crept up behind her and looked over her shoulder. A photo enlargement of his penis with the caption, "Scepter of the Gods," was sitting on it.

"I didn't hear the chime," Summer stated anxiously, then hurried to the door. "Crap. Someone took it. It's gone, Angel." She swung the door open and closed, checking it, then locked it.

Angel felt sick. "I don't believe this is happening. What the hell did I do to someone to make them fuck with me this way?"

"Oh, Angel, don't say that. You didn't do anything," Summer crooned, hurrying over to comfort him.

"I must have done something. I've gone almost ten years without anyone bothering me. I didn't think anyone even remembered my name or thought about those old films anymore. This is crazy."

Summer hugged him. Rocking him side to side, she pressed her face against his chest and squeezed him tight.

Right after Angel had called, Billy checked his in-box, then grabbed his car keys. He was going to submit the photos they had found the previous night into evidence, but now that there was another one, he decided to go get it and send it in with the rest.

Traffic was light. Billy pulled into the lot near Angel's car, then whistled a tune as he walked to the front of the shops. Just about to try the door, he looked inside and found his lover embracing that pretty blonde lady. A blast of jealousy hit him like the opening of a furnace door. Biting his lip, he knocked when he found the door was locked.

Angel looked up realizing Billy was standing outside the shop. "Billy!" he shouted, then nudged Summer back and hurried to open it. "Hello, babe." Angel kissed him quickly, noticing Billy staring at Summer. Having a feeling about what Billy may be thinking, Angel explained, "She was comforting me. The freak left another one inside the shop." Angel pointed. "On the counter."

Nodding, Billy didn't greet Summer when he passed by her to go to the counter. Angel felt slightly uncomfortably, but he could understand Billy's apprehension. After all, they'd only been on one date.

Always helpful, Summer rushed over to Billy and said, "I just found it. The guy, whoever he is, took our door chime so we didn't even hear him come in or out. I just found that there. I didn't touch it."

As she rambled, speaking quickly, Billy just nodded, staring down at the photo.

Angel whispered to her, "Why don't you get our coffees?"

"Oh. Okay." She skipped her way to the back room.

When she left, Billy looked over his shoulder in her direction, then at Angel. "You two close?"

"Not what you think. No. She's just a sweet girl." Angel leaned on the counter next to where Billy was standing. "So," Angel tried to laugh, "now my dick is a scepter. What next?"

"Neither of you handled this yet?"

"No."

Billy removed a folded brown envelope from his jacket pocket, then a pair of rubber gloves.

"You come prepared," Angel laughed.

"Always, gorgeous, always. Got a condom in my wallet, just in case."

Angel smiled at Billy's wink, glancing back to where Summer was approaching with their cups.

Taking his coffee from her, Angel thanked her as they both watched Billy slide the new photo into the envelope.

"Where's the other one?" Billy asked.

"In the office." Angel indicated the direction. "Summer, we'll be right back. Don't open yet. Hold off a few minutes."

"Okay, boss," she chirped.

As they walked back to the office, Billy asked, "How do you stand all that enthusiasm?"

"She's all right. I don't mind." Angel smiled.

The minute they entered the small back room, Billy closed the door behind them, set the envelope down on the desk and lunged for Angel hungrily.

Billy's hot mouth found Angel's and Billy's hands wrapped around Angel's head through his hair. Angel blinked his eyes in surprise and struggled to set the cup down so he could participate. Once Angel was able to get his hand free, he surrounded Billy's narrow waist and squeezed him close,

68

rubbing his hips against Billy's slacks.

"Oh...Angel, Angel..." Billy moaned. "I can't stop thinking about you."

"I'm flattered, really. I wish I could say the same. But, with so much crap going on—"

"I know, gorgeous, I know." Billy cupped Angel's face lovingly. "I'll work overtime. I'll stake out your house. I'll do anything I can."

Grinning in delight, Angel replied, "You're fantastic, you know that?"

"Christ, I want to fuck you right here on your desk...you get me so fucking horny."

At the comment, Angel peeked back at the closed door. Almost as if it was a signal, Billy began clearing the desk top off.

"No. Not for real," Angel gasped.

As if Angel needed more persuading, Billy enveloped him again, rubbing against him, using his tongue to tease his mouth and face.

Overwhelmed by the passion, Angel's head fell back as Billy's large masculine hands opened his tight faded blue jeans. When his lower half was exposed, Angel glanced back at the door, wondering what Summer would do if she walked in.

The mentioned condom was located and tossed on the desk. To Angel's amazement so was a small tube of lube. "Wow!" Angel was impressed. "You do come prepared."

"Bend over, you fantastic creature."

Stepping out of one leg of his jeans, Angel spread his legs wide, then leaned over the desktop. Hearing rustling behind him, Angel soon felt a hot cock knocking at his door. As he was penetrated, Angel closed his eyes and knew he'd never look at his office and desk the same way again.

Billy was in heaven. *This erotic fantasy just won't end.* Pumping his hips while wearing his suit and tie, his gun, and even his badge; screwing this incredible man, it was like living someone else's life. Not his.

Thrusting to a new level of pleasure, Billy pressed in deeply and came, closing his eyes at the intensity. With his cock still throbbing, he pulled out, catching his breath. Using a scrap piece of paper, he took off the condom, shoved it into the trash, closing his pants again.

Angel rolled over, smiling brightly. "Good one?"

"Oh, lover, you have no idea." Billy shook his head in awe.

"Excellent," Angel replied.

"Your turn." Billy knelt down and grabbed that incredible cock. Maybe it wasn't a scepter of the gods, but whatever it was, it was fantastic.

Going wild on Angel, shoving Angel's cock deep into his throat, so he, too, would come. Billy didn't stop until Angel nudged him gently after his orgasm as he recovered. Standing, helping Angel to fix his clothing, Billy wiped his mouth with the back of his hand and then just stared at Angel's beautiful face. "That hold you?" Billy said teasingly, as if this whole act was Angel's idea.

"I think so." Angel humored him.

"Good. You are insatiable, you know."

"I know!" Angel laughed, getting the joke.

"Right. Where's that other photo. Did we come on it? No. Good. The lab boys would notice."

"You're fucking hilarious, you know that?" Angel couldn't stop laughing.

"Yeah, that's me. Funny Billy Sharpe. You know that's my nickname down at the precinct?"

"Stop, I swear I'm going to piss my pants." Angel doubled over.

"Okay, enough comedy." Billy finished placing the paper into the envelope, then set it down on the desk. "Look. I don't like what's going on with this creep. He's getting a little bolder."

"Don't worry, I'll be careful."

"I mean it, Angel. I want you to be extra vigilant. I'll talk to the captain about getting someone assigned to this. I want a car around this shop and your house."

"You really think that's necessary?"

"Yes."

"I think that's overreacting. He hasn't made any attempts to hurt me. It's just this stupid paper crap."

"Maybe now..." Billy warned.

Summer knocked on the office door. "Angel? There's a line of customers outside. Should I open?"

"Oh. Yes. Sorry." Angel looked down at himself as if making sure he was decent, then opened the door. "Go ahead, Summer. I'll be out in a minute."

"Okay!"

When she left, Angel turned back to Billy. "Hey. You checking out my ass?"

"I am. Love that thing. Anyway, look, let me get all this new evidence to the lab. Call me all day long, every hour if you want. I need to know you're okay."

"I will. Thanks for coming by."

Wrapping around Angel's waist, Billy purred, "My pleasure."

They kissed quickly, then Angel walked him out.

As Billy left, he waved at Angel through the window. Angel felt his heart warm at the sight of him. When he walked back to the counter to be ready in case someone wanted a purchase, Summer giggled, "He's really cute, Angel. I'm

71

jealous."

"He is, isn't he?"

"Maybe he knows a nice cop to set me up with."

"I'll ask him," Angel humored her, then smiled as a man brought a book to the counter to buy.

Billy drove back to the precinct to update the report with the latest evidence. Sitting down at his desk, turning on his computer, he booted it up and searched for the right screen.

Detective Alexander wandered over to his desk. "What are you working on? Anything interesting?"

"Just that harassment case. I think our victim's got a stalker now."

"Oh?" Jay replied. "What's in the envelope?"

"Some photos of the victim that the suspect left around his shop." Billy typed as he spoke, getting the information documented.

"They going to the lab for prints?" Jay picked up one of the envelopes.

"That one is, not the other one." Billy gestured with his head to the one Jay was holding. Before Billy realized what Jay was doing, Jay had opened one of the envelopes and slipped out the paper inside.

"Jesus! This is that porn star guy! What was his name?" Jay held up the photo.

Pausing in his typing, Billy wanted to rip the photograph out of Jay's hand, but knew it would seem odd. "Loveday. Hey, could you put it back into the envelope?"

"Look at the size of his prick. Jesus. No wonder he's a porn star."

That angered Billy. He rose up, snatched the photograph out of Jay's hand and slid it back into the envelope.

"What's with you?" Jay reacted defensively.

"I've got some work to do. Ya mind?" Billy slapped the envelope down, sat on his chair once more, and continued typing. Without another word, Jay walked away. Peering up to see if he was gone, Billy felt very sorry for Angel. It seemed he would forever be held up for inspection and ridicule. It wasn't fair.

After he had finished the update on the report, Billy called the lab. "Hey, it's Detective Sharpe here in property, you got any results on case number…" he rattled off the information.

"Wait. I'll check."

Drumming his fingers on his desk, Billy checked the time and wondered how Angel was doing.

"Ya there?"

"Yes." Billy sat up.

"Two AFIS quality prints on the knife, but no hits."

"Okay, thanks. I'm going to submit another one I got today. I suppose it'll be the same." Billy glanced down at the envelope.

"The person's never been handled or printed. What can you do? If he's a criminal, eventually someone will bring him or her in and get them fingerprinted. Sorry."

"No. It's okay. Look, you got some good quality prints. That's something at least." He picked up the envelopes. "I'll see ya in a few minutes. I'll bring the new ones down."

"Okay, detective. We'll be here."

Billy hung up and rubbed his face. Getting to his feet, he checked he had everything he needed, then stopped by the lieutenant's office before going to the evidence department. Rapping his knuckles on the door, he waited, hearing his lieutenant's voice bidding him enter. Opening the door, Billy poked his head in. "Sorry to bother you, Ron."

"No bother. What's up?"

Stepping inside the office, Billy shut the door, standing

over the lieutenant's desk. "I've got a stalker case I'm working on, and I wondered if the captain would give me a uniform to watch over him."

"Him?" Ron asked.

"Uh, yeah. Our victim's a guy."

"Any threat of violence?"

Biting his lip in annoyance, Billy already knew what the answer would be to his query. "No. No violent threats."

"What are you basing your request on, Bill?"

What was he supposed to say? It was based on the fact that he loved this guy? "Just thought if we had someone around he wouldn't have to get harassed."

"You have a copy of the report?" Ron asked.

"I'll get you one."

"Leave it on my desk. I'll have a look at it, but unless there's an imminent threat to the victim, or something tangible, I doubt the captain will okay it. You know how short patrol is lately."

"What about an off-duty gig? You know, through the union?"

The look on Ron's face told him he was barking up the wrong tree. "What's your interest in this case? Why do you care so much? Is he a personal friend of yours?"

Allowing that much information to be public, Billy nodded, "Yeah. He's a friend. Never mind. I thought it was worth asking."

"Get me the report."

"Will do, L-T." Billy waved to him as he left his office, feeling heaviness in his heart.

By late afternoon Angel received a call. Taking it in his office, Angel sat at the desk and said, "Hello."

"Mr. Loveday?"

"Yes?"

"This is Mr. Fiennes, the vice principal at Oliver's school."

"Oh no. What's going on?" Angel felt his skin crawl.

"Oliver was caught fighting at lunchtime. I have him here in my office with the other boy. We're trying to make a decision on whether to suspend them both or not. I thought perhaps you'd like to come down."

"Yes. I'm on my way." Angel hung up and hurried to find Summer. She was ringing up a purchase for a customer. Angel waited for her to be finished before he approached her. "Look, Summer, I have to go to Oliver's school. Let's call it a day and close up."

"You sure? I don't mind watching the place for the last few hours." Summer looked around the empty shop.

"I don't want you here by yourself with that freak hanging around."

"I'm a big girl, Angel. I can handle it."

Fighting with his feelings on a decision, he finally said, "Fine." He handed her a set of keys. "You've seen me open and close a million times."

"Angel..." she sighed in exaggeration.

"Mary's right there if you need her, and Glynnis and Ray are next door."

"Go! I'll be fine."

"Call me. I want you to call me once you get home to let me know things are okay. Will you do that?"

"Yes, go!" She began shoving him to the door.

Reluctantly he left, jogging to his car and then racing down the highway. *Fighting? Now Oliver is fighting?* He could only imagine over what.

Storming down the hallways, his boot heels echoing on the linoleum, Angel found the correct offices and asked for his son. A secretary immediately showed him into the vice principal's office. When he entered he found Oliver, along with one other boy, sitting quietly side by side. Both young men looked up at him instantly. The second boy's expression sickened Angel. It was a knowing smirk he was beginning to see more often than he liked.

Mr. Fiennes stood up from behind his desk and extended his hand in greeting. Angel took it, shaking it.

Before Mr. Fiennes began, he instructed the two boys, "Go wait outside the office. No talking."

Oliver didn't meet Angel's eye, but the blond boy couldn't stop staring at him.

Once they left, closing the door behind them, Mr. Fiennes said, "Mr. Loveday, please sit down." He did, waiting for the bad news.

"Mr. Loveday," Mr. Fiennes began, "it seems an old photograph of you has circulated around the school. I'm very sorry."

Angel felt like throwing up. He sat still, not moving a muscle.

Mr. Fiennes opened the drawer slowly and removed the photo, handing it across the desk. It was one Angel had already seen, and he cringed in horror. Taking it reluctantly, he barely looked at it, folding it in half and placing it on his lap.

"We don't know which student brought it onto the school grounds. But Jerry, the young man outside with your son, taunted Oliver about it. So began the argument and battle."

"I see." A sensation of guilt crept into Angel's mid-section.

"We've had a discussion, and since Oliver was on the receiving end of the teasing, we will only give him a written warning. The other boy has a three day suspension."

"Fine. Whatever you decide."

"I would like it if you would have a chat with Oliver. Please tell him that if this happens again, he is to come to either myself or a teacher to resolve it. If he is caught fighting again, he, unfortunately, will be suspended, even if it is to defend you."

"I understand." Angel wanted to cry. He didn't have any idea how to handle this situation.

"That's all unless you have any questions."

"I do. Do you have any type of counseling available for Oliver?"

"We do. Do you think that would help?"

"Yes. Maybe he needs someone to talk to other than me." Angel looked back at the closed door, leaning over the desk to speak more privately. "This business about my past has just recently come up. I tried to protect Oliver from it, and I did for almost seventeen years. But, obviously someone found out, and now it's as if Pandora is out of her box. I can't talk to him about it; he's so angry with me. I've always had a good relationship with Oliver, Mr. Fiennes. But, lately, it's deteriorated to arguments and the silent treatment."

"I see. Well, I'll recommend he see the school counselor. You may even consider getting him private therapy to help him cope."

"I will. But odds are he'll refuse to go. Anyway, I've wasted enough of your time. Thank you for all your help and for not suspending Oliver."

Mr. Fiennes reached out to receive Angel's hand. "My pleasure."

Nodding in reply, Angel left the office and found his son sitting with the secretaries. Oliver glared at him, as if looks could kill. Angel nodded his head for Oliver to follow him, taking a quick peek at Jerry. The boy was snickering at him. Leaving the administrative offices, walking down the long hallway, Angel didn't say a word. He wanted to smack Oliver, to shout at him for being so stupid, but what he really wanted to do was get to his hands and knees and beg forgiveness.

The ride home was silent. Angel kept trying to think of a

way to discuss this subject without it turning into a roaring argument with more slamming doors.

When they arrived home, Angel allowed Oliver to enter first. Before Oliver disappeared into his bedroom and shut himself in, Angel stopped him. "Hey. Are you all right?"

Oliver sighed. "Yeah."

"You want to talk about it?" Angel gestured to the sofa.

"Not really."

"I guess I should thank you for defending me. If that was what you were doing."

A sarcastic chortle escaped Oliver's throat.

Angel reached out for him. "Come here. Please."

Giving into Angel's pleading, Oliver sat down. Sitting next to him, Angel held his hand and made sure Oliver looked him in the eye. When he had Oliver's full attention, Angel whispered, "I am so sorry. I'm sorry you ended up with someone like me for your father. Oliver, if I could erase my past I would do it in a heartbeat to help you. Please, forgive me."

"Never mind, Dad." Oliver looked away shyly.

"We used to be close, Oliver. We shared everything with each other. You know I would never do anything to hurt you. I love you. I do. I care so much for your well-being, I ache. I hate seeing you having to fight these idiots at school because of me. What can I do to help? Please, I'll do anything."

"Just let me deal with it."

"Okay. But, remember, you got off easy this time. Mr. Fiennes said the next time you are caught fighting he'll suspend you. Don't let that happen, Oliver. Don't ruin your education over some twit on the school grounds making fun of me. Promise me. Just ignore them."

"Can I go to my room now?"

"Oliver?" Angel touched his arm.

"I have homework to do."

"Okay. Go." Angel stared at him as he walked away, locking himself in his room again. Rubbing his face tiredly, Angel didn't know what else he could do. When the phone rang he grabbed it before Oliver picked it up, in case it was Billy. "Hello?"

"Hi, boss."

"Hi, Summer. Everything go okay?"

"Yes. No problem. I closed the shop regular time. I'm glad I did. We had a couple of good sales."

"Oh. Okay. As long as there were no problems closing on your own."

"Nope. Everything was just fine."

"Good. I'll see you in the morning? If you get there before me, let yourself in but don't open the shop until I'm there."

"Okay. I'll get us our coffees."

"Good girl. You're the best, Summer. Thank you."

"Is Oliver okay?"

Angel looked in the direction of Oliver's room. "I suppose."

"Anything I can do?"

"No. But thanks for asking."

"Okay, boss. See ya in the morning."

"See ya." Angel hung up, then stood, heading to the kitchen to fix something for dinner.

Billy checked his watch. About to leave his office for the day, he picked up the phone and dialed. When a young man answered, Billy jolted in surprise, then asked in a professional voice, "Yes, I need to speak to Mr. Gabriel Loveday, please."

"Hang on."

The phone was set down and Billy could hear a door open, and then a shout of "Dad!" A second later Angel picked up the phone saying hello. "It's me. Did your son hang up?" Billy whispered. A click was heard right after.

"Yes. He just did," Angel replied.

"How you doin', gorgeous?" Billy reclined in his chair. "Do I get the pleasure of your company tonight?"

"You mind if I take a rain check?"

Billy did, but could hear the strain in Angel's voice. "What's the kid done now?"

"He was caught fighting. One of those stupid pictures ended up at the school. He was defending my honor, such as it is."

"The school?" Billy sat up in his chair. "How the fuck did it end up there?"

"Hell, I don't know. Maybe one of the kids was walking around Redondo near the shop and pulled one off a tree. Christ, there were dozens of them hanging around."

"Huh." Billy tried to understand the connection to the photo appearing in a high school. "Anyway, I'm on my way home. Can I call you when I get there? I can't really talk dirty to you here." Billy spied someone walking by his desk.

"Sure," Angel chuckled. "Call me before bedtime."

"I will." He hung up, then straightened up his desk and headed home.

After a late dinner, Angel showered, then relaxed in his bed with a new novel before he went to sleep. When the phone rang, he grabbed the extension off his nightstand quickly, saying, "Hello?"

"Hey…were you sleeping?"

"No, Billy. I was just reading a little before bedtime. How are you doing?" Angel set the book on the nightstand and stretched out his naked legs under the crisp sheets.

"I forgot to tell you earlier…we got a few prints off the

knife, but nothing was matched to it. So, our little villain isn't in the system yet."

"Is that a good thing or a bad thing?" Angel tried to find some humor in it.

"Well, both. It's good because he's not a known felon, but bad because we don't know who the pecker is."

Angel smiled in delight, loving Billy's accent. "Where the hell were you born? You're not a native to California, are you?"

"Chicago. You can still hear it in my accent? Christ, I've been livin' in LA for almost fifteen years."

"I still hear it, hot stuff. And I love it." Angel looked over at his closed bedroom door. "You know, I'm hard as a rock."

"Don't tell me that! I'll be coming over, running code, lights and sirens blazing."

"I can't help it. I kept thinking about the way you molested me in my office earlier today." Angel reached his left hand between his legs.

"Molested you? Is that what I did?"

"Oh yes, you bent me over that desk and shoved your big hard dick into my ass..." Angel stroked his cock, wanting Billy's mouth on it again.

"Christ, you keep talkin' like that and I'm going to have to jerk off."

"So? I am. Got my hands on myself as we speak."

"Jesus! Wait. Let me strip and get in bed. Will you wait?"

Hearing the excitement in his voice, Angel laughed, "Yes, I'll wait." He lowered the sheets down to his thighs and made himself more comfortable. A minute later the breathless detective got back on the line. "Ya there, gorgeous?"

"I'm here. You naked, copper?"

"Yeah, naked, in bed, got my legs spread, and thinking of your tight ass."

"Good, very good," Angel crooned.

"Talk to me. Talk to me, Angel…"

"All right…" Angel lit up with excitement. "Like I was saying, you had me bent over that desk in my office…"

"Yeah…"

"My ass naked and ready for your cock…"

"*Oh*, Loveday…"

"And you pushed in…so fucking deep it makes me shiver…and my cock grew rock hard from it…from you sticking that cock of yours in me…" Suddenly Angel heard a familiar gasping sound. Smiling in pleasure, he waited. "You there?"

"Oh, yes… Christ. I can't hold it thinking of you."

"Your turn?" Angel made himself more comfortable on the bed and gripped himself tighter.

"Yeah…uh…I want to suck that cock of yours. You know? I just want to shove it into my mouth, down my throat…I want to taste your come…"

Angel increased the speed of his hand, then arched his back and came, closing his eyes as Billy's seductive words echoed in his ears. After a pause, Billy asked, "Did it work?"

"Yes…wow." Angel looked down at his white spattered chest.

"You are too much, Angel."

"I wish you were here." Angel looked for something to use to clean up. He found a tissue and dabbed at the spill.

"Ditto. How about tomorrow?"

"Yes. I do need to see you." Angel tossed the tissue on the floor.

"Good. I'll let you get some rest. Call me in the morning and let me know what you plan on doing."

"Okay, baby. You got it."

"Good-night, Angel."

"Good-night, Billy." Angel hung up, then made a move to get cleaned up in the bathroom. Catching something in the reflection of his dresser mirror, he spun around to his window and spotted a silhouette of someone who had been watching him.

"I don't believe this!" he shouted, grabbing his jeans and jumping into them. He dashed to the back of the house. Bursting through the screen door of the porch, the crescent moon illuminating the whitecaps on the ocean waves, Angel rushed to the side of the house and looked around for anyone lurking.

"Dad?"

Angel perked up and hurried to the sound of the voice. "Oliver?"

"Dad?"

It was faint, blown away on the stiff cold breeze. Angel couldn't figure out where it was coming from. "Oliver? Are you out here?"

"Dad!"

Completely confused by the direction of the voice, Angel looked over the edge to the bottom of the small cliff. "Oliver?"

"Help, Dad!"

"Oliver!" Angel climbed down the rickety ladder, sand showering down with every step. As he descended, a rung broke under his weight and he fell, reaching the sandy bottom with a thud. Pausing a moment to see if he was hurt, Angel stood up, brushing sand off his naked arms and chest, and began shouting for his son. Suddenly a light shone on his face from above. Shielding his eyes from the glare, Angel shouted up, "Oliver? Is that you?"

No answer returned. The light scanned down his body.

"Oh no," Angel moaned as it dawned on him he had been duped. "Who the hell is that?" he shouted, the light blinding his eyes. "All right, enough!" Furious, Angel went back to the ladder and tried to climb up. All the rungs had been cut and they snapped as he stepped on them. Moving back, his hand blocking the light, he shouted, "What the hell are you trying to do? What do you want from me?" Eerie silence followed. The wind felt icy cold on his naked skin. "Look, whoever you are, throw down a rope, will ya? It's fucking cold!" He could swear he heard the receding sound of laughter in the wind.

The light faded. "Hello?" he called out. Feeling the chilled air that blew off the ocean, Angel tried to climb the broken ladder once again. Pieces of the worn wood fell apart in his hand and he kept sliding down to the sandy bottom. Cursing in fury, he jogged down the beach to the neighboring house. A large wooden fence protected the property from intruders. Angel banged on the gate but knew the sound would be blown away and useless. His fists clenched, Angel walked back to that cliff where the ladder to his home stood. He sat down against the wall of sand and curled up into a ball to protect himself from the cold, then lowered his head to his knees and held back his sobs of frustration.

Chapter Seven

The alarm sounded and Oliver woke, yawning and rubbing his face. Kicking off the blankets, he scuffed to the bathroom to shower and get ready for school. After he was dressed he listened at his father's bedroom door and didn't hear any movement. Shrugging indifferently, he prepared a bowl of cereal for himself and ate it, checking the wall clock, making sure he made it to the bus on time.

Oliver rinsed out his bowl, grabbed his book bag, then his keys. He paused, considering saying goodbye to his dad before he left. He thought about what he might face in school in the day ahead after the fight he had with Jerry and changed his mind. Slamming the door, he left, walking to the bus in a foul mood.

Billy arrived at work early. Sitting down at his desk, he checked the contents of his in-box for new cases, prioritizing them. Before he began his work, he called Angel's home number. When no one answered he tried the shop. "Hello, Ms. Thompson? It's Detective Sharpe, is Angel there?"

"No, detective. He isn't. I was getting a little worried about him. I mean, he's usually a little late, but not this late. I even bought coffees and everything, and luckily he gave me the key last night because…"

As she rambled incessantly, Billy began to panic.

"Okay...okay, look, let me drive by his place. All right?"

"Oh! Could you? Yes. Maybe he forgot to set the alarm. Tell him everything's fine here. I'm okay by myself for a while. Can you tell him that?"

"I will, Ms. Thompson. Let me go." Standing, Billy walked around the desk as he hung up the phone, then jogged to his car.

Restraining the urge to run code to Angel's house, Billy sped over the winding streets with horrible thoughts going through his head. If anything happened to Angel he'd feel personally responsible for it, and just the thought of it was killing him.

Screeching to a halt in Angel's driveway, seeing his Camaro parked in front of the garage, Billy hopped out and knocked on the door. No one answered. He shouted Angel's name, then tried the knob. Moving to the front window, Billy looked in, pushing on the glass, hoping it was open. It wasn't. Banging the windowpane, he shouted Angel's name again. "Please be in the damn shower," he muttered, hoping that was the reason he couldn't hear the door.

Walking to the corner of the house, Billy had a look at the fence and thick shrubbery. Swearing under his breath, he took a deep inhale for strength, then ran and leapt onto the barrier, holding the top and scrambling to get over its height. Jumping down to the other side, Billy paused when he noticed footprints. Prints that seemed to have done exactly what he just did. Pausing, studying them curiously, he kept clear of them, still following their path. They stopped at a north side window. Looking in, Billy could see it was a bedroom. An empty bedroom. He kept moving to the back of the house. The ocean came into view. "Angel!" he shouted out, just in case Angel was somewhere in the back of the property. A very faint sound returned. Billy rushed to the edge of the lawn and looked down.

His teeth chattering from being out in the elements all

night, Angel heard someone calling his name and assumed it had to be Oliver. He answered back, trying to be heard over the incoming tide. When he spotted Billy looking over the edge, he felt instant relief. "Billy! Get a rope!"

"Ya got one? In the house?" Billy shouted down.

"Yes! Look in the oak box in the porch!"

Billy nodded and hurried off.

Rubbing his arms for warmth, Angel hopped up and down trying to get the feeling back into his numb legs. A rope tumbled down the edge near the ladder. Angel tugged on it and felt a secure hold. He began climbing up, using what was left of the ladder and clinging to the rope. As he neared the top, Billy reached out his hand. Angel gripped that warm hand and was hauled up to the top of the small cliff.

When he was on firm ground, he noticed the look of concern on Billy's face. "Thanks."

"Get inside." Billy wrapped his arm around Angel's shoulders and escorted him in. "Christ, you're ice cold. Where's the shower?"

"In there." Angel tilted his head in the direction, then shouted for Oliver and checked his room seeing he had already gone.

Billy led him into the bathroom, turning on the water. When steam was billowing out of the stall, Billy helped Angel slide his jeans off, then gave him a hand stepping into the tub.

Angel moaned in pleasure at the heat. Once he had thawed out, he noticed Billy watching him.

"Ya gonna tell me what the hell happened?"

"Yes. Let me just wash and get out of here." Angel quickly shampooed his hair and then shut off the water. Billy held a towel for him, wrapping him in it, then followed Angel to his bedroom.

Angel dropped the towel, finding some clean clothing to slip on. "Last night, during our phone call…"

Billy sat down on the bed and nodded that he was listening.

"...well, right after I, you know, did it with you, I was getting out of bed to wash up when I noticed someone standing at that window." Angel pointed. "I could see his reflection in the mirror."

Billy nodded.

"I ran out, trying to catch the fucker. The moment I got out there, I heard what I thought was Oliver calling my name. I don't know how the creep did it, but it did sound like my son. I thought Oliver had fallen off the edge and may be hurt. So, like an idiot I climbed down to see. The asshole cut through all the rungs on the ladder. I was stuck down there all fricken night."

Billy's intense stare didn't change.

"When I first fell, the creep put some kind of spotlight on me. I'm telling you it was fucked up. Really fucked up. I froze my ass off down there. I was digging in the sand to try and keep warm." Angel shouted, "Summer! The shop!"

"Don't worry. She said she had it under control," Billy assured him. Slowly he stood and embraced Angel, rocking him.

Angel felt so much comfort in the touch he wanted to cry. "Thanks for looking for me. I mean that."

"Why the hell didn't your son look for you when he didn't find you here?" Billy leaned back to see Angel's face.

"I told you about the fight he got into yesterday. Maybe he was still angry with me. I don't know."

"You sure your son has nothing to do with what's going on?"

"I'm sure. He may be confused, but he's not nuts. No way."

"Do you feel all right? Do you want me to take you to your doctor?"

"No. No, I need to get to the bookshop. I can't leave Summer there by herself all day."

"I can drive you." Billy pushed Angel's damp hair back from his face.

"And pick me up? That's not necessary."

"What if I insist?"

Angel's chest warmed at the care he was receiving. "Keep that up and I may just begin to like you a whole lot, Detective Sharpe."

"Oh? Am I on the right track to winning the beautiful Angel Loveday's heart?"

"Yes, you are." Angel smiled adoringly at him.

"When you give me that look I want to screw you." Billy drew closer, kissing Angel's jaw and neck.

Shivers ran down Angel's back. Closing his eyes he imagined them naked, squirming on each other. "Shit, I have to get to work."

"Call her." Billy kept kissing Angel's neck, his ear, his cheek.

"Yes. Let me call her. Hang on...don't go anywhere..." As he walked to the phone, he dragged Billy with him, making sure he kept kissing him. Angel dialed the shop and Summer answered quickly. "Summer? It's me. I am so sorry."

"Did you oversleep?"

"No. Long story. I'll tell you when I come in. Are you okay?"

"I'm fine. It's dead."

"You sure?"

"Yes. It's really desolate out there. I think the weather is changing and keeping people off the beach."

A warm male hand squeezed Angel's crotch. He inhaled and closed his eyes again. "Ah...okay, you mind if I get there a little later?"

"Nope. I'm fine."

"Okay. I'll see you in about an hour."

"Okie dokie!"

Angel hung up, then spun around and connected to Billy's lips. Inhaling his cologne, lapping at his mouth, cupping his rough jaw, Angel was in heaven. Billy untucked Angel's shirt and began feeling his chest, pinching his nipples. Angel squirmed in delight as a hand dug into his tight jeans. When fingers wrapped around Angel's cock he opened his eyes and breathed, "Get in the bed. Now."

In a swift movement, Billy picked Angel up in his arms and carried him to the bed. Setting Angel down gently, Billy stood back, staring at him as he undressed.

Angel's eyes were wide as he watched that suit and tie come off, the holster and gun, then the black slacks. Wriggling out of his own tight clothing, Angel waited, naked, as Billy removed everything he was wearing. Seeing Billy's eyes dart to the window behind the bed, Angel sat up, made sure the blinds were drawn tight, then located the rubbers and lube to have within reach.

Once he was reclining on the bed again, he noticed Billy standing at the foot, gazing down at him. "Everything all right, detective?"

"You are so amazing looking."

"Am I?" Angel smiled.

"You haven't changed in twenty years."

"Oh, I wish I could believe that." Angel laughed, flattered.

Slowly climbing down on the bed, Billy wrapped around him, sniffing and kissing Angel's face and hair.

"What do you want, baby?" Angel purred, stroking Billy's hair back from his forehead.

"You, you, you..."

"You have me. You know that." Angel smiled, kissing his

nose.

"How's your ass?"

"Fine. You want it?"

"Not too soon?"

"Nope." Angel grinned wickedly.

As if his comment lit more of a fire in Billy, he went wild, rubbing his hands all over Angel, between his legs, under his arms, behind his head, down his thighs, everywhere at once.

The caressing was making Angel crazy. Gently Billy urged Angel to his hands and knees. Hearing Billy preparing himself behind him, Angel tried to look over his shoulder, then smiled happily and rested his head on the pillows.

"Ready, gorgeous?"

"Yes." Angel felt a lovely drowsiness and wished after lovemaking they could fall asleep in each other's arms. That sensation soon changed to sensual pleasure.

Billy couldn't get enough of him. The craving to be inside Angel's body was as urgent as his craving for air. The feelings that were growing for Angel, Angel the man, instead of Angel the icon, were so strong, Billy imagined for the first time in his life, he may actually be falling in love. That adoration of a celebrity film star that he had always admired and lusted for had morphed into a deeper, richer feeling of the desire to protect, to care for, to provide for. Almost as if he had a woman's nesting urge. He wanted so much to settle down with this fabulous man, grow old with him, chat in front of fires, take long walks on the beach…was he nuts? Falling in love with Angel Loveday?

"Yes, yes!" Billy shouted as if answering his own question as he thrust into Angel deeply. Hearing Angel giggle, Billy leaned over his bottom and gripped that world famous cock. "Who you laughing at?"

"Ah!"

Billy grinned, loving the sound of pleasure coming from Angel as he jerked Angel off with the same timing as his hip thrusts. Soon conversation stopped and only panting breaths and grunting filled the room. Arching his back, Billy came, closing his eyes, but made sure his hand kept moving until Angel was satisfied. Hearing his orgasmic moans, knowing them now by heart, Billy smiled in pleasure and rested his head on Angel's back, catching his breath.

"Oh, baby…that was intense." Angel disengaged himself from Billy's hips, rolling over.

Kneeling up on the bed, Billy looked down at Angel's naked body and then sighed. "Christ, you're like a drug."

"A late drug. I have to get to the shop."

"Yes. I suppose screwing on city money isn't very nice either." They climbed off the bed and washed up quickly in the bathroom.

As he got dressed, Billy said, "Look, I've spoken to the lieutenant about this case. I don't think he thought it was serious enough for a patrol car to be assigned here, but now, after what happened last night…"

Angel zipped his jeans, found a rubber band for his hair, putting it back into a ponytail. "I don't need a security guard."

"Bullshit." Billy clipped his holster in place.

"Look, Billy, though the guy has done stupid things, he hasn't tried to harm me."

Billy knew that would be the same argument he would get from his supervisor. "Live with me until we catch this guy."

"I can't. What about Oliver?" Angel tucked in his shirt.

"He can move in, too."

Angel smiled adoringly. "It's a wonderful thought. I appreciate it. But Oliver would never do it."

"Does he even know about this stalking business? Or about us?" Billy knew the relationship between Oliver and Angel was strained.

"No," Angel said softly, as if he were embarrassed.

"Well, tell him! Tell him what the hell you're going through!"

"I can't. Look, let me go. I've been gone long enough."

"I'm driving you." Billy finished dressing, slipping on his suit jacket.

Angel stood in front of him and fixed Billy's tie. "What if you get a late case? I'll be waiting around for you."

"Angel," Billy admonished.

"I'm not weak. I can defend myself." Angel kissed Billy's chin, then walked to the living room.

In frustration, Billy followed him. "You won't let me protect you."

"From what?" Angel asked seriously. "He's just being a pest."

"Oh? Leaving you to freeze all night on a beach? A pest?"

"I've got to go." Angel grabbed his keys and headed to the door.

Billy stopped him, pulling him roughly into an embrace. "Call me. I'll be worried sick about you if I don't hear from you."

"I will."

"Dinner tonight?" Billy released him.

"I'll let you know."

Hating the reluctance but knowing it was because of Oliver, Billy just nodded his head and followed Angel outside.

"Summer, I am so sorry." Angel hurried into the shop and looked around. Only one customer was browsing.

"No problem. It's been really dead. It's raining, isn't it?"

"Just started." Angel kept walking to the back office. "Let

me drop off my jacket and then I'll be right back."

"Okay."

Angel draped his leather jacket over the chair, then looked around the desk casually. An image flash of Billy screwing him on it washed over him. Savoring it, he joined Summer as she stood by the counter, sighing deeply at finally being able to stop moving.

"So? What happened?"

"I was trapped on the beach all night. Never mind. It's too stupid."

"No! By that stalker-guy? Oh, no, Angel. Did you call the police?"

"Billy found me. He came to my house and got me off the damn beach. I froze my nuts off. I was only wearing a pair of jeans."

"I can't believe this. I'm so glad you're all right. When are they going to catch this guy?"

"I don't know, Summer. I really don't know."

"Uh, I'm not trying to change the topic or anything, but, are you coming to my Halloween party?"

"Oh, that…well."

"Please? You promised!"

"I don't remember promising." Angel dreaded it.

"Oh, come on. It'll be fun. There's a ton of people coming. At least just pop in for an hour or so. Please?"

Smiling tightly, Angel knew it would upset her if he didn't go. He just had too much on his mind at the moment.

After school, Oliver set his books down in his room and foraged for some food. A half hour later, he heard his father come home. Looking up from his homework, he said hello and waited as his dad took off his coat and dropped his keys on the table.

"You okay?" Angel asked.

"Yeah."

"No problems at school?"

"No…"

Angel nodded then went to the kitchen.

"Ah, Dad?"

"Yes?" Angel poked his head out again.

"Did you mention you were invited to a Halloween party?"

"Yes. Summer is having one Saturday night. Why?"

"I don't know. I was thinking about it and maybe I will come after all."

"Oh? Cool. I didn't want to go, but if you come, I will. She's been nagging me for weeks about it."

"Ah, where does she live again?"

"Wilmington."

"No, I mean her address."

"Why do you need that? I'll drive us."

"Oh, uh, I was just thinking of asking one of my friends to meet me there. You think she would mind?"

"Are you kidding? You want to go there with one of your friends?"

Oliver nodded, trying to keep a serious expression in the face of his father's doubt.

"I think I have her address written in my little phone book. You know the one. It's on my night table."

"Cool. Thanks."

As if it was an afterthought, Angel asked, "Which friend?"

Not wanting to commit to any names, Oliver shrugged. "I don't know yet."

Nodding, Angel went back to the kitchen to start dinner. The moment he did, Oliver searched for his address book and located it on Angel's nightstand. Just before he brought it to his room, he noticed something on the floor. Leaning down to take a closer look, he realized it was a wrapper to a condom. Glaring at his father through the wall, Oliver headed to his bedroom, closed the door and picked up his phone. "Hey, Per? I got the address. You going to crash the party? Good."

Winding down after dinner, Angel checked on Oliver, found him on his bed strumming his guitar, and headed to his own room. Sitting down on the bed, Angel picked up the phone and dialed Billy's mobile number. As it rang Angel noticed something on the floor. He grabbed the wrapper crushing it into a small ball. When a service picked up, Angel left Billy a message. "Hey it's me. Call me when you get a chance."

Hanging up, Angel stood, then brought the wrapper to the kitchen trashcan and buried it deep in the garbage so Oliver didn't see it. When the phone rang, Angel hurried to the extension in his bedroom so he could speak privately. Once he picked it up, he heard Oliver had already answered. Oliver asked Billy, "You my dad's boyfriend or something?" Angel was about to interrupt when Billy said, "No. Just a friend. Is he there?"

"I'm on the line. I got it, Oliver." Without a word, Oliver hung up. "Sorry about that."

"No problem. You okay? Anything happen at work?"

"No. It was blissfully uneventful."

"When can we see each other again?"

"Tomorrow? It's Friday night. I'm assuming Oliver will have plans."

"Good. My place?"

"Okay. My turn to treat you to dinner?"

"Whatever you say, gorgeous."

Angel smiled. He wanted Billy with him. As the pause grew and they just listened to each other breathing, Billy whispered, "I miss you, too."

"Damn, you're good. A mind-reader, as well?" Angel laughed.

"Maybe. Maybe I was just hoping you felt the same."

"I do." Angel cuddled the phone, wishing he could nestle into Billy's neck. When he looked up, Oliver was glaring at him from the doorway. "Hold on, Billy." Angel cupped the telephone. "You need something?"

"I'm not an idiot. You don't have to lie to me."

"Shit, hang on." He spoke to Billy, "Let me go. I have to talk to Oliver. I'll see you tomorrow. Okay?"

"All right, babe. Don't let him bully you."

"I won't." Angel hung up, meeting his son's furious expression. "Okay. You want the truth?" Angel asked. Oliver, arms crossed firmly over his chest, nodded. "Fine," Angel began, "I'm being stalked by a lunatic. Detective Billy Sharpe, is helping me with it. We do like each other. All right?"

"You two already screwed."

"Why do you say that?" Angel felt a cold chill.

"I found the stupid wrapper to the rubber. You screwed in that bed, didn't you?"

"Oliver…" Angel sighed, standing up to go after him when Oliver stormed away. Stopping Oliver's bedroom door from slamming shut, Angel stood at the threshold as Oliver lay down on his bed in a huff. "Yes, we screwed. I really like him."

"You're disgusting."

"What? Since when did I raise a homophobe?"

"Just leave me alone."

"Oliver, why can't we talk this out? Why does it always have to be left angry and unresolved?"

"Because you're a whore! All right? My dad's a slut who screws men, all right?"

"I am not a slut! How dare you? Do you realize I haven't

97

so much as dated since your mom died? She died when you were seven, Oliver. Do the math."

"I know when Mom died. You don't have to remind me."

"Good. And those men I was with in the films, they weren't my boyfriends. Okay? So cut me some slack. I haven't had nearly the amount of men in my life you're imagining."

"Yeah, right."

Angel threw up his hands in exasperation. "I can't win."

"Just leave me alone."

"Oliver..." Angel pleaded.

"I said leave me alone!"

Angel left the room, closing Oliver's door quietly. Sitting down on his bed, he rubbed his forehead, wishing he could somehow fix everything.

Chapter Eight

Meeting Perry in the hallway of the school, Oliver stuffed some books into his locker and then shut it with a metallic bang. "So," Oliver asked, "what are you going to be for this Halloween party?"

"Changed my mind."

Looking over Perry's shoulder, Oliver noticed Len standing down the hall at his locker. Oliver waved to him when he looked his way. Bringing his attention back to Perry, Oliver asked, "Why aren't you going now?"

"I just thought it would be too boring."

"That's what I thought. I was wondering why you were even interested in the first place." Oliver nudged Perry. "Let's see if we can go over to Len's place later on to practice."

Perry shrugged, following Oliver to where Len was waiting.

Near lunchtime, Angel took a break and closed himself into the office in the back of his shop. Picking up the phone, he dialed Billy's mobile phone number and sat down comfortably in the chair behind his desk.

"Detective Sharpe," Billy said when he picked up the phone.

"Hello, detective," Angel whispered seductively.

"Hello, gorgeous. You okay?"

"I'm fine. Just wondering about our plans for tonight." Angel toyed with the phone cord.

After a deep exhale, Billy replied, "Anything is fine."

"I know a nice Italian restaurant near the Fashion Center."

"That's fine."

"Are you okay?" Billy's voice seemed strained.

"Yeah, nothing you have to worry about. So, what time? You want me to pick you up?"

"Either that, or I can meet you at your place."

"Okay. Come to my place and I can drive us from there."

"You sure you're all right?" Angel sat up in his chair.

A long pause followed, then Billy muttered, "The lieutenant wants to see me in his office. That usually means bad news. Never mind. See ya about five thirty?"

"I'll be there." Angel hung up, still thinking about the conversation.

Billy straightened a few papers on his desk, then rose up, buttoned his suit jacket and made the long walk down the hall. He rapped his knuckles on the office door and heard his lieutenant bid him enter. Poking his head in first, Billy found him seated at his desk. "You wanted to see me?"

"Sit down, Bill."

Obeying his order, Billy sat down, opening the button on his suit jacket again.

"I've read this report," the lieutenant said, lifting a corner of it off his desk. "If it's not a property crime, why are you handling it?"

"It came across my desk as a property crime. It was only after talking to the victim that it needed re-classifying."

"Then it shouldn't be with you any longer. Send it to the

crimes against person unit."

"I just figured since I started investigating it—" Billy was growing angry, trying not to let it show.

"It's not our case now. And I also notice its crossing jurisdiction. Some of the incidences were Redondo's sector, not ours."

"I know. I've sent them copies."

"What's going on, Bill? This, Loveday, is he really a friend of yours?"

"He is." Billy sat up straighter in the chair, trying to project an air of confidence.

"Angel Loveday?" the lieutenant sneered, "that lewd Eighties porn star?"

Billy could feel the heat of rage quickly come to his cheeks. "Ron, no disrespect intended, but I would like to remain on this case. I don't want to pass it off to some schmuck in another department who'll let it lay in their in box because they don't like the victim."

"Why do you think that will happen?" The lieutenant reclined in his seat, waiting, as if he needed convincing.

"Look at your reaction," Billy snapped, then tried to calm his voice. "Listen, Ron, it's one fricken case. Loveday is in trouble and I want to help him. We don't usually stick that tightly to protocol around here. If cases overlap we help each other out. It's not that unusual."

It appeared the lieutenant was still considering.

Billy decided to go for broke, knowing how politically correct the department had become in recent years. Leaning over the desk as if to speak privately in an already private office, Billy let go a sentence he never thought he would ever reveal. "He's my lover, Ron."

It took a moment to sink in, then the lieutenant whispered in reply, "Are you telling me you're gay and dating Angel Loveday?"

"Yeah." Billy reclined back and watched the information get digested.

After a brief shake of his head in disbelief, the lieutenant seemed to get completely flustered. "I had no idea. Okay. No problem. I get it now."

Billy had to hide his smile. It worked like a charm.

"Fine. You do what you need to do. Get Redondo involved. You want me to talk to them?"

Standing, grinning down at the lieutenant, Billy assured him, "That won't be necessary. I got it handled."

"Okay. Just let me know if there's anything I can do."

"I will, L-T. Thanks for understanding." Billy buttoned his jacket again before he left the office.

"No problem. I'm just glad you let me know. It all makes sense now."

Pausing, his hand on the doorknob, Billy had a last thought. "The other guys don't know. I just assume keep my private life private."

"I understand. They won't hear it from me."

"Thanks, Ron." Billy smiled at him, then left. As he walked back to his desk, he was whistling happily to himself.

Friday night closing time had finally arrived. Angel began locking up the safe and shutting off lights. He checked his watch and called home. No one answered. Leaving a message for Oliver, Angel then hung up and met Summer at the front door. "Everything off?" Angel asked.

"Yup." Summer zipped up her jacket as she stood next to him.

They both hurried outside quickly after Angel set the alarm. He locked the door, jiggled the handle, pocketing the keys. "Right. Let's go."

They walked to the parking lot together. The wind had

picked up as the clouds moved in from the ocean. Streetlights illuminated the cars remaining in the parking lot. Once Angel unlocked his car door, he shouted to Summer, "See you in the morning."

"See ya!"

Sitting down behind the wheel of his car, Angel was about to put the key in the ignition when he noticed something crammed under his windshield wiper. Getting out, seeing Summer's car leaving the lot, Angel stood next to his fender and raised the windshield wiper up to get the object out. It was a small photograph, jammed and bent down almost under the lip of his hood. Unfolding it to look at it, his heart once again beating in his chest, he found it was a snapshot of him taken the night he was left on the beach. The angle was from above and he was lit with a spotlight or flashlight. Investigating the area around him to see if he was being observed at the moment, he found nothing suspicious. The lot was almost vacant except for a few lingering shoppers climbing into their cars. Getting back into his Camaro, he grumbled under his breath, set the photo on his seat to give to Billy, and started the car.

Checking the time, Billy showered and changed into some casual clothing. Leaning over the mirror in the bathroom, he inspected his jaw to see if he missed any spots when he shaved, then ran his fingers through his damp hair. A dab of cologne and he was ready for Angel. Clicking off the bathroom light, he did a quick walk through of his home to make sure everything was in its place, slipping his wallet and keys into his pocket. Removing his gun from the shoulder holster, Billy placed it into a smaller leather one that clipped to the waistband of his jeans. Making sure he had his badge and ID card with him, he then picked out a light jacket from his closet to cover the presence of the gun.

When his doorbell rang he felt his heart skip a beat and hurried to open it. Just the sight of Angel standing in the light of the porch was enough to ignite Billy's passion. Opening the door for him, Billy said, "Hello, Angel. Come in."

"Hi, Billy."

Billy paused, looking at his expression, touching Angel's long hair where it flowed down his shoulders. "What happened? I can always tell when something's happened."

Without a word, Angel handed him the photograph.

Feeling sick as he stared at it, Billy shook his head and asked, "Where did you find it? Left in the shop again?"

"No. Stuffed under the wiper of my car."

"It's from the night you were stuck on the beach, isn't it?" Billy set it down on a side table.

"Yes."

"You want to sit down?" Billy offered. "Can I get you something to drink?"

"What have you got?" Angel sighed, taking off his leather jacket.

"I'm well stocked. Name it."

"Scotch?"

"Have a seat. I'll bring it to you." Billy left to get him his drink. As he poured two small glasses of scotch, Billy was so furious with the harassment Angel was enduring he could scream. A glass in each hand, Billy returned and sat next to Angel, handing him one.

After a sip, Angel said, "If he had a camera that night, then he took one of me jerking off. I bet he has one of me in my bed."

Billy wanted to tell him it wasn't true. He wanted to comfort Angel and tell him he'd be okay. But not knowing what the stalker would do next, Billy couldn't find it in himself to lie. Instead he set his glass down on the coffee table and wrapped his arms around Angel.

With a deep sigh of relief, Angel rested his head on Billy's shoulder. "Why won't he leave me alone? What the hell did I do to deserve this?"

"Nothing. You did nothing."

Angel set his glass down beside Billy's on the table, cuddling against his warm chest. "You watch. Photos of me masturbating will be next on his list."

"Maybe not," Billy replied, rubbing Angel's back softly. "I looked through that window when I climbed over the fence that night. All I could see was the reflection in the mirror. You can't actually see the bed. And I'm only guessing here, but if he had a photo that good, why didn't he put that on your windshield? Huh? No. He didn't get that one. He got the only one he could that night."

Angel tried to feel some reassurance from those words. "Maybe you're right."

"I am." Billy set back from him and pushed Angel's long hair away from his face. "You want to eat in? I can call for a pizza."

"You mind?" Angel asked, not wanting to disappoint him.

"Not at all. What do you like on it?" Billy stood, taking off his light jacket.

After sipping more scotch, Angel faced him, seeing the gun at his waistband. "Ah, anything. I'm not picky. Just no anchovies."

"Got it."

When Billy disappeared into the kitchen, Angel gulped down the liquor, looking around at the minimalist style décor. The house had a nice open airy feeling to it that he liked. His tiny cottage felt claustrophobic at times. But of course Billy didn't have beachfront property. Getting to his feet, Angel brought both their glasses with him to the kitchen. Billy was standing with the telephone to his ear and an open yellow pages directory in front of him on the table.

"Yeah, I'd like to order a pizza...delivered?"

Angel smiled sweetly at him, setting the glasses on the counter by the sink. He stood behind Billy and wrapped his arms around his waist.

As a set of masculine hands smoothed down the front of his abdomen to his crotch, Billy lost his train of thought. "Uh...what did I say? Oh, yeah, pepperoni, no, that's it." Those hands grew bolder, cupping over his balls, massaging them lovingly. "A half hour? Yeah, that's fine." Billy nodded, then thanked the man and hung up. Standing perfectly still, he enjoyed Angel's fingers as they explored his anatomy, closing his eyes to savor the touch.

Growing hungry for sex as he grew hard, Billy didn't know what Angel intended to do in the short time they had before the pizza arrived. Knowing they could have a long slow bout of lovemaking after they ate, Billy asked softly, "How late can you stay tonight?" as he removed the gun from the waist of his pants and set it next to the glasses on the counter.

"Ten?" Angel replied, digging inside Billy's jeans to touch skin.

Tensing up as Angel's fingers wrapped around his cock, Billy felt like passing out it was so intense. It was as if Angel had magic fingers and everything he touched turned Billy orgasmic. "If you keep that up, I'm going to cream my pants."

A low chuckle answered him.

The stroking became bolder. Billy glimpsed down. Angel's hands were deep inside his denim, testing the strength of the material. Behind him, Angel was humping his ass in hard but very slow thrusts. Angel's head was resting on the back of his neck, close enough for Billy to hear Angel's breaths and tiny sounds of passion. Pressing back in time with Angel's pumping rhythm, Billy closed his eyes again and savored this slow dance of carnal desire. The pressure of Angel's hard cock against his ass, Angel's hot hands stroking him just enough to keep him on the edge and going insane, and Angel's lovely whispering voice beginning to play like music to his ears.

"I want you…" Angel breathed. "I need you…"

A wave of pleasure washed over Billy's skin almost bringing on a climax. He forced himself to hold back, gritting his teeth, then relaxed once he felt in control again. Allowing his head to fall back against Angel's, Billy rubbed his cheek on Angel's long hair, yearning for Angel's lips and tongue, but those were out of reach.

The sensation of floating, hovering above the planet in some perpetual state of euphoria, washed over Billy. He could dance like this for hours. Even though they hadn't changed their rhythm, it slowly felt as if it was escalating to the point where at any moment, they would face one another, tear off each other's clothing, and fuck like dogs in heat on the kitchen floor.

Billy had no idea how long they were lost, swooning, but when the doorbell rang he was disappointed that the time had passed so quickly.

With some tugging, Angel removed his hands from Billy's pants. As Billy blinked his eyes and tried to get back to normal, he tucked in his shirt and took his wallet out of his pocket. Muttering as he answered the door, Billy breathed, "I don't even want the fucking pizza. I just want to screw."

He heard Angel burst out laughing, having overheard him. Billy looked back at him and shook his head as he opened the door.

Chapter Nine

Standing in Oliver's room, Angel stared down at him as he lay on his bed. "You sure you've changed your mind and you don't want to go to Summer's party?"

"I'm sure." Oliver barely opened his eyes.

"You said one of your friends was going—"

"I said I'm sure!"

"No need to shout at me, Oliver," Angel chided in irritation. "Fine. You have her number if you need to contact me. I shouldn't be home late. I was only planning on staying a short while." Angel waited. Oliver didn't answer. "What are you doing tonight?"

"Nothing."

"So, you're just going to stay home?"

"Probably."

"You don't need me to drop you off anywhere?"

"Daaaaad!"

"Fine!" Angel held up his hands in surrender. Leaving Oliver's room, Angel grabbed his keys, then the stupid cowboy hat which went with his cowboy outfit. Closing the front door behind him, Angel sat in his car and attempted to start it up. The ignition sounded flat, as if the battery was dead. "Oh, great," Angel sighed, tried the key once more, heard nothing, not even a click. Climbing out in frustration, he thought about calling Summer to tell her he wasn't going to come only to hear the disappointment in her voice. Shaking his head at the futility, he went back inside, grabbed his motorcycle keys, heading out to the garage to pull the bike out. Stuffing the hat into one of the saddlebags, Angel straddled the heavy Harley Davidson, kicking it into action, the noise seeming to ricochet off the surrounding hills. After it had warmed up and the idle had settled down, he pushed it off its kickstand, heading south to Wilmington via Highway 1.

Forgetting how much he enjoyed the bike since he usually only rode it in the summertime, Angel felt exhilarated as he flew over the open road. Twenty minutes later he was parking in front of Summer's house. The street was flooded with cars, so he wedged the bike length-wise between two parted bumpers. The minute he shut off the bike he could hear the music from inside the house spilling out onto the street. Through the sheer curtain he noticed a mob of people. "Holy shit," he mumbled in surprise. But Summer did warn him it would be a big affair. Just as he was walking up to the front door, he remembered his hat and went back to the bike to get it. Working on it to get it back into shape, Angel then popped it on his head and resumed his walk to the door. Reaching out to ring the bell, Angel stopped short as someone opened it for him before he rang. A ghoul with blood caked on his face smiled sweetly. His ugly make-up was an odd contrast to his nice expression.

"Howdy, partner."

Angel shook his head at the disguise. "How do you say hello to a zombie?" Angel asked.

"Hell, I don't know."

Passing him by, Angel got his first look at the interior. No cliché Halloween decoration was lost on it. Pumpkins, skeletons, spider webs, black cats, witches, every kind of cutout, or hanging creature was jammed into the space of this tiny three bedroom Tudor. Angel didn't recall the last big party he'd been to. But the memory it was evoking made him believe he was glad he gave them up.

A black light was lit and causing everyone to glow. The living room television was playing *The Rocky Horror Picture Show* as music from the stereo blasted loud rock and roll. Angel wanted to find Summer, say hello, then slowly make a quick exit. As he searched room to room, the stares he was enduring were unnerving. Did they all recognize him? Is that why they were ogling?

When a hand found his bottom, Angel spun around to confront the assailant. A very drunk Summer was giggling at him. "Look at you..." Angel shook his head. "Leather? Since when are you into S and M."

"There's a lot you don't know about me, cowboy." She tapped the brim of his hat. "I'm so glad you're here. Is Oliver with you?"

"No. He changed his mind at the last minute. Christ, Summer, do you really know all these people?" Angel tried to be heard over the noise.

"No, not really. Everyone just brings a friend. Isn't it great?" She looked around, sipping her glass of pink liquid. "Why didn't you bring that detective-guy?"

Hating the idea of subjecting Billy to this type of punishment, Angel just smiled and said, "He was busy."

"Too bad. Oh, there's a ton of booze there if you want it." She pointed to a large ice chest along side a table of hard liquors.

"Can't drink. I brought the bike. You have anything else? Like soda or juice?" Angel asked, leaning close to her ear so she could hear.

"There must be orange juice there. Just help yourself..."

"Thanks, sweetie."

"Mingle!" She shoved him.

When she vanished into the throng, Angel made his way over to the refreshment table. He located a plastic cup and poured orange juice into it.

"Howdy, Tex."

Twisting around, Angel found a woman dressed as a fairy. "Hello." He smiled politely.

"Is that a gun in your pocket or are you glad to see me?"

"I expect I'll hear that line all night," Angel replied, laughing, and looking down at his toy gun.

"No doubt, good-looking. You want to dance?"

He peered over her shoulder at the whirling dervish taking place in the living room, then shook his head. "You mind if I pass?"

After he said it, she spun around to see the chaos for herself. "Looks daunting."

"Yes, it does. You mind waving your wand and making them all disappear?"

She thought about it and began shaking her glittering stick around. Once she did they both waited. "Doesn't work like in the old days." She frowned.

"Oh, well." Angel smiled.

"Catch you later, Tex."

He waved at her, noticing a chair had opened up in the kitchen near the threshold to the living room. Sitting down on it, Angel placed his orange juice next to him on the food-covered table. As he relaxed he admired all the creative costumes, some of which were very elaborate and obviously took a lot of time to create.

As he panned the two rooms, which he could see from his vantage point at the joining of them, he noticed someone standing in the corner of the living room. There, being very still and calm in the clamor, was a person draped in black with the Scream mask covering its face. The mask was staring at him.

He couldn't tell if the occupant was as well. It gave him the creeps more so than several other monsters that were roaming around.

The fairy reappeared. Angel smiled at her pleasantly. It seemed she had been dancing. Sweat beaded her forehead and upper lip. "You need to sit down?" he asked her with the intention of giving up his chair.

"Thanks." She plopped down on his lap, surprising him. "It's crazy out there."

Agreeing with her, when Angel nodded the brim of his hat hit her in the arm. Taking it off, Angel shook out his long straight hair, searching for a spot to put his hat. The fairy-woman took it, setting it on her lap.

"Damn, you're gorgeous."

Angel laughed shyly. "Thanks. Ah, you're pretty, too."

"I wasn't fishing for a compliment. Anyway, you know the person whose house this is?"

"Yes. I work with her." Angel looked once more into the corner of the living room, but the person in the Scream mask was gone.

"Oh. Where do you work?"

"I own a little bookshop down on Redondo Beach."

"Cool. You should be a movie star."

Angel averted her intelligent eyes before she figured out who he was. He had no idea of her age since she was covered in sparkling make-up.

When he shifted under her, she asked, "You need to get up?"

"I'm just looking for my drink," Angel replied, peering around the table.

"You want me to get you something?"

"No. I had some orange juice here a minute ago." Sitting up higher on Angel's lap, the fairy reached behind him and set it down where he could see it. "Is that it?"

He raised it to his nose, taking a sip. "Yup. Thanks. Ah, you mind if I stand up?"

She got off his lap and said, "Nope. I'll save your seat."

"Thanks." He winked at her then took his hat from her. Not wanting to stick the cowboy hat back on his head because it was driving him crazy, Angel looked for a place to set it down. Pausing in the hallway, he finished the orange juice, tossed the cup out into a trash bag, then placed his hat on top of the refrigerator, where it was out of everyone's way.

Looking for the hostess with the leather spiked heeled boots and whip, Angel found her dancing the Time Warp along with the movie that was playing on the screen behind her. As he watched, a slight wave of dizziness washed over him. Thinking it was warm in the room, he loosened his collar and rolled up his cuffs. A cold sweat broke out on his skin. Angel imagined going outside for a breath of fresh air, but he never got that far. Another current of something powerful washed through his body. Reaching back for the wall, he heard someone murmur, "Too much booze. Better let him lay down."

Angel shook his head, trying to clear it. A stranger opened a bedroom door and sat him on the bed. As quickly as they brought him in, they left.

The room felt cool and dark. Angel kept rubbing his eyes and face, trying to focus. A shivering tide of dizziness cascaded over his body making him feel completely disoriented. He lay back on the bedspread and tried to stop his head from spinning. His tongue felt thick and slow, and his limbs began tingling and feeling numb.

A movement of the door caught his eye. It opened and closed quickly. A latch clicked.

Angel couldn't see who had come in. Then as if in a nightmare, the glowing face of the Scream mask came into his view. Edvard Munch's creation come to life. In his head Angel was speaking, but nothing was coming out. His body was slowly becoming paralyzed. Never, in his forty years of existence, had he take a drug this strong. And he had taken many.

In the silence inside the room, Angel could hear the heavy breathing behind that rubber mask. Deep inhaling, sucking wet breaths, slurping drooling sounds that were so repugnant, Angel wanted to cower in fear. Hands wearing black cotton gloves opened the buttons of his denim shirt. Angel wanted to shove those hands back, but he couldn't. Watching, as if out of his own body and overlooking this dreadful event, he knew immediately he had once again fallen prey to this fiend.

His shirt was spread wide. More wet sucking noises followed. Grotesque sounds. Sounds of a lecherous demon fondling himself in a dark theater, a pedophile ogling school children. His belt was unbuckled. Those dark hands opened the top button, then his zipper. The faded blue denim material was spread wide over his lower abdomen. A hand reached into his jeans and exposed him.

Angel was in agony. Begging his arms to move, praying for his legs to function, it was as if he were under anesthesia for surgery and had somehow come awake as they cut.

Something cold and wet ran across his chest all the way down to his waist. He imagined being eviscerated, carved up and mutilated. Shivering in terror, Angel tried to open his eyes wider and raise his head to look, but he couldn't.

A white flash of light blinded him. Another and another. Angel cringed and felt his head aching with each searing strobe of light.

That gloved hand fondled his body, then tucked his cock back into his clothing, zipped him up, buttoned his shirt, tucked him in. All the while that sickly slurping sound, drool oozing out of a wet mouth; the leering pervert, getting its jollies from being in control.

Once his clothing was completely intact, Angel heard the click of the door latch. It opened, a whoosh of air hit his face and then the door closed and it was dark and still in the bedroom again, the noise of the party still going on outside.

He didn't know how long he lay there. But, slowly his limbs began to function. Angel struggled to move his arms. When he could use them he propped himself upright on the bed. His head ached instantly, like a migraine. Sitting still, allowing the feeling to come back to his legs, Angel touched his face, trying to get back to normal. With a great effort he made it to his feet. Walking out of the room, hearing some noise, but no music, Angel wondered how long he had been out. When he entered the living room, a cheer went up from the occupants. Angel was so disoriented he couldn't figure out what was going on. Summer was clapping, whistling at him, everyone was staring at him strangely, with big silly smiles on their faces. Finally his attention was drawn to the television set. *Lust* was playing. People were trying to shush each other to listen to the dialogue. There, on the screen, Angel was standing naked in a bathtub as an older, shabbily dressed man with a potbelly and a cigar, and a woman in a red teased wig, scrubbed him with a soapy sponge.

"Oh, god, no...Summer," Angel whined, his head killing him. "Why the hell is that on?"

"I don't know. Someone must have brought it. It's not the one I have." More viewers shouted for her to be quiet. She walked across the packed room, and stood next to Angel. "Don't worry. Everyone's drooling over you."

"Please. Shut it off. Please."

"Are you okay?" she asked in concern.

"I just need some air." Angel tried to walk through the living room. Dozens of costumed party-goers were crammed tightly, watching his naked body on the television set. After managing to get out, Angel felt sick. He stood next to a large thick oak tree on her front lawn and threw up, holding his stomach in agony.

Crouching down, trying to decide if he was going to die,

Angel narrowed his painful vision at the sight of that Scream mask lurking along the side of Summer's house watching him. "Who are you?" Angel tried to shout, but he knew he didn't have the strength.

It vanished quickly into the darkness.

Covering his face in anguish, Angel burst into tears. It was too much and it was finally getting to him.

Billy sat in front of his television drinking a beer and checking the clock. He knew Angel had that Halloween party to go to, but he also knew Angel wasn't interested in staying there long. Bored, longing to hear his voice, Billy called Angel's house and was annoyed when Oliver answered. "Yeah, ah, is your dad there?"

"No. He's at a party."

"I know. I was just checking if he was back."

"No. Not yet."

"Okay, tell him I called...wait. Ah, do you have the number he can be reached at over there?"

A long irritated breath preceded, "Hang on," as if it were a supreme effort.

Billy imagined punching the kid. Finally Oliver came back, rattling off the number. "Thanks," Billy said, and was hung up on. Mumbling profanity under his breath, Billy called Summer's number. When she answered the noise in the background was amazing. "Hello?"

"Summer? It's Billy. I was just wondering if Angel was still—"

"Billy! I'm so glad it's you!"

Billy sat up. "Why, what's wrong?"

"Angel must have ate something funny. He's really sick."

"What's your address?" Billy wrote it down frantically. "How sick. Did you call an ambulance?"

"No. He's just thrown up. I don't know what's wrong with him."

"I'll be right there. Stay with him! You hear me?"

"Okay."

Billy knew it. He wanted to go, but no, Angel said it was crazy to put him through such a stupid party. No, he would be fine! *Well? Are you fine, Angel?*

Flying over the roads with his dashboard blue and red light flashing, Billy raced through red lights and stop signs, his heart pumping as he panicked. Screeching to a halt, double-parked in front of Summer's house, Billy couldn't believe the number of cars on the street. Rushing to the front door, he spotted Angel sitting on her porch, his head in his hands. Billy's heart sank. "Angel."

Hearing that voice, Angel raised his head to Billy's look of concern. "What are you doing here?"

"I called Summer. She told me you weren't feeling well."

"I need to go home. I brought my bike. I was waiting for someone who could give me a lift. I don't feel up to riding."

Billy reached out his hand.

Angel took it and walked gingerly with him to his car.

"Christ, what the hell happened to you?" Billy opened the car door for him, then just noticed a shiny chrome Harley parked between bumpers.

"I must have had something that made me sick."

Shaking his head, Billy closed the passenger door for Angel, then sat behind the wheel. "What did you eat?" Billy started them moving northbound.

Angel thought hard for a moment. "Nothing."

"Drink?"

"Ah, orange juice."

"That's it? Orange juice? Angel, someone slipped you

117

something."

Angel tried to remember. He couldn't. Crouching over his lap, almost doubled over from the illness, Angel rubbed his face, exhaustion creeping up on him.

"I should take you to the ER," Billy suggested.

"No. No, I just want to go home. Please, Billy."

In the silence that followed, Angel felt Billy's hand reaching for his. Angel clasped it tight, holding on for dear life.

When they came through the door of the cottage, Billy had his arm around Angel's waist, helping him walk. Looking around for Oliver, Billy hoped the kid had left or was asleep. No one needed a confrontation at the moment. Billy helped Angel to his bedroom, setting him down on the bed. "You want a glass of water?"

"Yes, please." Angel nodded as he started to unbutton his shirt.

Billy acknowledged him and hurried to the kitchen. He found a glass in one of the cabinets and bottled water in the fridge. Rushing back again, Billy paused at the door. Angel was in tears, covering his face. Crouching down in front of him, Billy asked, "What's wrong? Baby, don't cry."

Very slowly, Angel sat up, opening his shirt wide on his chest. Billy read the word *Filth* written in what appeared to be red lipstick across Angel's body. His heart sank in his chest. "Oh, Angel...what the hell did he do to you?" Billy took Angel into his arms and held him tight.

Over Billy's shoulder Angel sobbed, "It's what I am, Billy...it's what I am."

"Stop that shit. Come on. Let me get you cleaned up." Gently, Billy helped Angel to his feet. Billy wanted to document it for evidence, but he just couldn't imagine putting Angel through any more misery. As they exited the bedroom and turned right to the bathroom, Oliver's door opened.

Oliver poked a sleepy head out and asked, "What's wrong with Dad?"

"He just needs to shower and rest, Oliver." Billy walked past him quickly.

"Too much to drink, Dad?" Oliver shouted sarcastically.

Before he could prevent it, Billy had Oliver by the scruff of his neck, lifting him off of his bare feet. "Listen, punk, your father's been through enough shit already, okay? So, lay the fuck off!" Billy shoved Oliver back, into his room.

"All right, Billy," Angel chided, "don't take it out on him." Then he shouted to Oliver, "Go back to bed. I'm fine."

Before he closed the bathroom door, Billy looked over his shoulder seeing a different, more concerned, expression on Oliver's face. Glaring at Oliver, Billy shut the bathroom door for privacy focusing on Angel once again. Slowly he helped Angel remove his shirt and tiny plastic toy gun and holster, and his tight faded jeans and boots. When Angel stood naked, Billy could see the writing had gone all the way down his body to his pubic hair. Furious with the violation and assault Angel had endured, Billy tried to keep his face a mask to prevent upsetting Angel even more. He reached in and turned on the shower, then helped Angel into the tub. While Angel wet down, Billy took off his jacket and shirt so he could reach in and help scrub that blood red word off Angel's skin.

Soaping up a sponge, Billy began washing Angel's chest. As he did, he was surprised his own tears were falling down his cheeks. Wiping them away roughly, Billy was mortified to be perceived as weak. When he peeked up at Angel to see if he noticed, he found Angel was staring at him endearingly. "Soap must have gotten in my eyes," Billy mumbled.

Knowing Angel didn't believe a word, Billy paused in his scrubbing as Angel cupped his face with his wet hands and brought Billy to his lips to kiss. It was just a loving peck, but it meant everything to both of them.

The marring word washed down the drain, Angel shut the

taps and stood dripping as Billy found a terry cloth bath sheet to wrap him in.

With Billy there, Angel felt safe once again. "Stay," Angel whispered.

"What about Oliver?"

"It's okay."

Nodding, Billy followed Angel to the bedroom, closing the door behind him. Angel dropped the towel, then picked up the glass of water and drank it down thirstily. He was feeling better, but still had a slight headache. In the mirror's reflection he could see Billy set his gun on the dresser, then undress. Angel watched him get naked, smiling adoringly at him. Once they were both ready, they crawled into the bed and shut off the light, wrapping around each other, trying to fend off the goblins and spirits of the night.

Chapter Ten

Sunday morning the sunlight struggled to enter the dim room through the blinds. Billy slowly came to the surface of reality, stretching out his back and arms. Seeing strange surroundings, it took him a moment to remember he was at Angel's beachfront cottage. Immediately he rolled over to have a look at his lover to make sure he was all right. Angel was sleeping soundly, his long hair running in brown rivers over his shoulder and across the white pillowcase. Smiling at his handsome face, Billy gently brushed a lock of hair back from Angel's forehead. At the touch, Angel stirred, opening his eyes with a blink.

"Hello, gorgeous," Billy purred.

"Good morning," Angel hummed back.

"How do you feel? Any residual effects from last night?"

As if Angel was just remembering something, his brow furrowed in concern. "A Scream mask."

"A Scream mask?" Billy echoed.

"Yes. The person who drugged me was wearing a Scream mask. I remember that now. I first saw him or her in the living room at Summer's house. They were standing very still...wait a minute." Angel hopped out of bed and opened his closet door.

Sitting up on the bed, Billy watched curiously, trying not to be distracted by Angel's fantastic naked body, and waited.

"I thought so!"

"What?" Billy asked. "What's going on, Angel?"

Stepping out of his closet, Angel pushed his hair back from his face and said, "Last Saturday I found someone had been digging in my closet when I wasn't around. There's a box under my clothing with all my old videos and some memorabilia from that time in my life. *Lust* is missing."

"What am I suppose to assume from that information?" Billy bent his knees tightly to his body, wrapping his arms around them, trying to understand what Angel was talking about.

"Last night, at Summer's place, someone put *Lust* into the video player. Summer said it wasn't her copy. Someone else had brought it there."

"And?" Billy waited as Angel climbed back on the bed.

"Well, whoever stole it from my closet must have been there at the party."

Billy's expression dropped. "You didn't mention a break in. When were you burglarized?"

"No. I wasn't. I thought at the time that one of Oliver's weird friends did it."

"What?" Billy shouted, then calmed down. "Why am I just hearing about one of Oliver's weird friends now? Angel if you have a suspect, tell me."

"I don't know if I do. It's just that Oliver has been hanging around this odd boy named Perry."

"Perry? Perry what? When was he here last? Why didn't you mention him before?"

"Calm down, Billy. Let's not jump to any conclusions."

Billy faced Angel on the bed and grabbed his hand. "You said somehow the photo made it to the high school, remember? I couldn't figure out the connection then, but I do now."

"Where are you going?" Angel asked as Billy climbed out

of bed.

Slipping his trousers on, Billy replied, "To ask Oliver some questions."

"No. Wait..." Angel jumped out of bed to stop him.

"Wait for what?" Billy yelled. "Angel, if some high school punk-ass kid is responsible for all this crap, I'm going to find out."

Before Angel could prevent it, Billy stormed across the hall to Oliver's bedroom. Without knocking, he barged in and flipped on a light. Oliver woke with a start and shielded his eyes from the glare.

"Hey, kid, tell me about this freak Perry." Billy stood over Oliver's bed, imposing and tall.

"What? What are you talking about?"

Angel showed up at Oliver's door, listening.

Turning to see Angel standing there in just a pair of jeans, Billy addressed Oliver again. "What's Perry's last name?"

"I don't know. Leave me alone. Get out of my room."

Billy took a menacing step closer to Oliver, imagining grabbing him and throttling him. "He drugged your father last night at the fucking party, Oliver. He fucking assaulted him. What's his fucking name!"

"Billy, all right," Angel admonished. "No need for that."

"No need?" Billy roared. "This punk asshole has been stalking and harassing you for more than a week, and there's no need?"

Oliver sat up and asked, "What? What's going on, Dad?"

Angel sat on Oliver's bed to speak calmly. "We're not accusing anyone, Oliver. But it seems to me that this whole business started when you brought Perry to the house."

"What whole business? What are you talking about?" Oliver looked up at Billy quickly, then back at his father.

Billy was about to explode. "Don't you even know what

your father has been dealing with?"

Angel stood up and approached Billy. Whispering, Angel said, "Why don't you go wait outside and let me talk to Oliver."

About to object, Billy read the need in Angel's eyes and relented. "You talk first. If you get nowhere, my turn."

"Okay." Angel appeared to be humoring him.

Billy headed to the bedroom door, giving a warning glare at Oliver as he left the room. Hearing murmuring coming from behind the closed door, Billy wandered to the kitchen and found some ground coffee to make a pot. Once it started dripping, he was drawn to the back of the house and the view of the ocean. Opening the back door, he stepped out onto the porch and inhaled the fresh sea air. The western sky was still dusky from the long dark night. The wind was brisk and chilling. Seagulls floated on the stiff current as whitecaps cut at angles across the deep turquoise sea.

Just as he was walking back inside to get a cup of coffee, he noticed Angel coming towards him. "Well?"

"He said Perry couldn't have done it."

"And? You believe him?" Billy followed Angel into the kitchen where Angel took two mugs out of the cupboard.

Angel filled both cups with coffee, handing one to Billy.

"Angel," Billy breathed out in frustration. "How the hell does Oliver know what this kid, Perry, has been up to? Look, did you at least get a last name?"

"No. He said he doesn't know it." Angel handed Billy the carton of milk.

Shaking his head at the absurdity of this conversation, Billy poured milk into his cup. *Fine, I'll find out for myself.*

Angel knew he was frustrating Billy, but the thought of a seventeen year old being capable of so much hostility didn't seem possible to him. Angel sipped his coffee staring at Billy, trying to read his thoughts. Instead of continuing in the same vein, Angel asked, "You have plans today?"

Billy seemed to snap to attention. Shaking his head. "No. You?"

"No. I'm free. Why don't we climb back in bed for a while? It's only seven thirty."

Nodding, Billy set his cup in the sink, gesturing for Angel to lead the way. Angel also set his cup down, then grabbed Billy's hand and brought him back to his bedroom. Once they were inside, with the door closed, Angel stripped his jeans off and climbed back in bed. When he did, he noticed Billy looking at something closely.

"You okay?" Angel asked.

"Yes. I just noticed you have a television and VCR in here."

"And?" Angel laughed.

"You'll get upset. Never mind." Billy took off his pants and laid them on the chair with his other clothing.

As Billy climbed back under the covers, Angel asked, "What? You can ask me anything. You know that."

"It just seems out of line considering everything you've been saying and going through."

Angel snuggled closer to Billy, smiling at him. "Just ask."

A blush came to Billy's cheeks as he whispered shyly, "Well, you said you had all your videos? In the closet?"

Angel started laughing. "Oh, don't tell me!"

"Well? You know how hard I've tried to get my hands on them? They're all out of print and I have to hunt around for used copies. And even those are impossible to find."

"You really want to watch one of those horrible old films?" Angel knew he should be angry, but he wasn't. He was very flattered and amused knowing Billy was crazy about him.

"I've never seen *Shame*. I've wanted to ever since I knew it existed."

"Now?" Angel stifled his laughter.

"It'll be the foreplay to very hot sex," Billy advised clinically, "that I can promise."

Shaking his head at the playful smirk on Billy's face, Angel climbed out of bed, took the video from the box, then stuck it into the VCR and hit the play button. Taking the remote control onto the bed with him, Angel climbed back under the blankets and snuggled close to Billy as he sat up eagerly to watch.

The music brought Billy back to his youth. How many times had he gone to the backstreet cinemas to see those Plimpton films? All alone, hoping no one recognized him, sitting with other solo men, all seemingly wearing trench coats and sunglasses as if admitting they were fans of these cult films was a crime. Even on the small screen, Billy felt the effect of the powerful charisma of Angel Loveday. Placing his arm around the real Angel, Billy salivated, dying for Angel's clothing to come off, which did sooner rather than later in these art house films.

A back alley, money being exchanged, Angel was on his knees in front of a customer, sucking the man's large dick. Billy's own cock was incredibly hard watching it. It was an undercover sting. The customer was a cop, but he still wanted this macho stud to suck him. It was only after the cop had come in Angel's mouth that he flashed his badge and told him he was under arrest. *Weren't these movies great?* Five men in uniform materialize from all over the alley. Angel is placed against a graffiti-covered brick wall. Three of the stunningly handsome officers are feeling every part of Angel's body up simultaneously; inside his trademark tight, torn, faded, blue jeans, up his naked torso, through his hair. The look of ecstasy on Angel's face is phenomenal. A deal is struck. Lots of butt fucking and cock sucking on Angel's part and he gets off with just a warning.

Billy was already so hot he had to come. These Plimpton movies did it to him every time. Twisting to look down at Angel's face as he too stared at the television screen, Billy leaned down to kiss Angel's hair.

Angel peered up at him.

"I'm already so fucking horny I could die." Billy tilted his hips up, his erection making a hump in the sheets.

Angel burst out laughing. "It's only been on for ten minutes!"

"I know! I told you they drive me crazy. You...you drive me crazy." Billy lowered down and stroked back Angel's long hair. Cupping Angel's face, Billy kissed him, moaning at the incredible irony of seeing his heartthrob on film, only to have him there to touch in real life. If only every teen's fantasy could come true like that.

Angel's hands gripped him under the sheets. The heat and force of the hold sent chills over Billy's body. Instinctively he began pumping into Angel's palm. Occasionally peeking at the movie, seeing Angel now completely naked, strutting around the movie set as if he were a god, Billy closed his eyes and came. He knew it would take nothing, nothing at all.

"Wow!" Angel tried to cup the warm sperm. "That was quick."

"I know. I'm telling ya, looking at those old movies drives me nuts."

A wicked gleam came into Angel's eye. Slowly he began licking the come off his hands. Billy lit up in delight. "Oh, you nasty boy. Get the fuck over here." Billy wrapped around Angel and rolled on the bed with him, grinding his hips against Angel's. Sitting up over him, straddling Angel's body, Billy had a good look at Angel's face and torso, then lowered down and sucked Angel's cock, deep and hard. Angel arched his back and groaned in pleasure. With the sound of the movie star Angel giving his best orgasmic performance in the background, the real life Angel grunted and came, shivering as he did.

Billy lapped at his cock in pleasure, then raised his chin so he could stare at Angel, something he couldn't get enough of. Oh, he loved Angel all right. Loved him so much he could burst.

When they were both showered and dressed, Angel suggested a stroll on the beach. Just before they walked out the back door the phone rang. Angel picked it up and said hello.

"Hi, Angel. I just wanted to see if you were okay."

"Oh, hi, Summer. Yes. I feel much better."

"What do you think brought that on?"

"I think someone may have put something into my orange juice." Angel watched Billy as Billy stared back at him.

"No way. None of my friends would ever do something like that to you."

"You didn't know everyone that was there. And speaking of that. Did you know the person in the Scream mask?"

"What Scream mask?"

"The short person all in black with the glowing Scream mask on." Angel and Billy didn't stop staring at each other.

"I don't remember that. Oh, well. Why? Is it significant?"

"Yes. But if you don't remember, never mind. Is my bike still out front?"

"I'll check." A pause followed, then she said, "Yup. Safe and sound."

"Good. I'll come by and get it later."

"Why don't you just get it Monday? I can pick you up."

"No. It's okay. Billy will take me over to get it later on."

"Okay. Oh. I have that copy of the tape, *Lust* that was playing. No one claimed it, so I told them I would give it back to you."

"Thanks, Summer. Believe it or not I think it's my copy. Someone took that video from out of my closet last Saturday."

"Man. None of this is making any sense to me. But, okay, if it's yours you can have it back. Oh, and your cowboy hat was left on top of my refrigerator."

"Yes. That's right. Will you be around later?"

"I'm not going anywhere. Any time is fine."

"Okay, Summer. See ya." Angel hung up and met Billy's eyes once again. "You can bring me by later to get my bike, right?"

"Yes. Are you feeling up to riding?"

"Yeah, I'm okay."

"You still want to take a walk on the beach?" Billy asked.

"Yes. Let me just get my jacket."

Billy nodded, waiting in the back porch.

Oliver listened at his door. As the conversations faded away, he picked up the phone and dialed. "Hey, Perry."

"Hey."

"What are you doing?"

"Nuthin'"

"So, ah, what did you end up doing last night? Anything good?" A long pause followed.

Finally Perry asked, "How's your dad?"

"Why?" Oliver asked suspiciously.

"No reason."

"He's fine. Why shouldn't he be fine?"

"I said no reason."

"You want to get together and practice?"

Perry groaned in annoyance and said, "You don't think

anything's going to come out of us three playing crappy music, do you?"

"No. I just thought it was fun." Oliver didn't understand Perry's attitude. It was as if Oliver couldn't say anything right.

"Fun? Yeah, whatever. So, what's your dad doing today?"

"Why the hell do you always ask about him? You know, Per, someone's like stalking him. He's really been going through a hard time."

After a callous laugh, Perry replied, "Is that right?"

"Yes. You have any idea who could be doing it?"

"No. Why ask me? There are millions of people out there who know about him. Porn star Loveday. The guy with the big dick."

"Shut up, Perry," Oliver snarled.

"Well, you asked. Anyway, gotta go."

"Will you be in school tomorrow?" Oliver asked.

"Don't know. See ya."

Oliver heard him hang up, then set the receiver down and thought about it. *Could it be Perry? Nah.*

Walking hand in hand on the wet sand, Billy raised his head to gaze at the long stretch of vacant beach. In the wild wind no one was out and about on it. Once they had come to a barrier of stone they turned around to head back, beginning to feel the chill.

"Penny for your thoughts?" Angel asked Billy.

"Hmm?" Billy turned to look at Angel, smiling at him. "Just trying to piece things together. It's just like a puzzle, Angel, and in the end it all falls into place."

"The end? You have any idea when that will be?"

"No. But Monday morning, I'm going to do more investigating. I have some fresh ideas." Billy was going to head directly to the high school and find out about "Perry".

"Anything you want to divulge?"

"You don't worry about it. You let me take care of it."

"Okay, Detective Sharpe, anything you say," Angel teased in a serious voice.

"Get over here." Billy wrapped him into an embrace and kissed him passionately, loving Angel's tongue. "That mouth of yours makes me want to come."

"I know." Angel giggled.

"Want to go back and screw?"

Bursting out laughing, Angel replied, "Anything you want."

"Good. Give me some of that," Billy reached between Angel's legs.

Angel darted away and started sprinting down the beach. In hot pursuit, Billy was trying to pinch Angel's ass as they ran. The two of them were laughing like children in the playground.

When they finally found the right property, they had to use the rope that was attached to the frame underneath the porch to climb up. After they stood at the top, Billy said, "You know. I can help you fix that ladder."

"Okay. Soon. Not today."

"Whatever you want, gorgeous," Billy purred, following Angel into the house, feeling like a love-sick teen.

By late afternoon Angel had Billy drive him to pick up his motorcycle. Feeling healthy and well again, especially after a full day of sexual fulfillment, Angel stared contentedly at the passing cars and homes as Billy turned down Summer's street. Immediately Angel spotted his bike out front, glad it was in one piece.

Billy parked and climbed out of the car, meeting Angel on the sidewalk. "Angel," Billy shouted as Angel headed to Summer's front door. Pausing, Angel spun around to his call.

Backtracking, curious as to what was wrong, Angel noticed Billy nodding to the Harley, pointing at it as he approached it.

"What?" Angel felt slightly uneasy thinking something could have happened to his prized possession.

"That look familiar?" Billy pointed to the sissy bars.

There, hanging over the chrome was a mask. The Scream mask. A wave of panic washed over Angel at the sight. "Great, just fucking great."

Billy shouted, "Don't touch it. Let me deal with it."

Nodding, Angel waited as Billy opened the trunk of his unmarked patrol car and removed something. Wearing a pair of latex gloves, Billy picked up the mask and placed it into an evidence bag.

"It won't end." Angel rubbed his arms.

"Oh, yes it will," Billy muttered as he brought the mask to his car and dropped it into the trunk.

Angel heard someone shouting his name from behind him. When he looked over his shoulder, Summer was waving from her front door. "Billy, Summer is there," Angel let him know. Billy acknowledged him and then met him on the pathway up to her door.

"Hiya, Summer." Angel hugged her in greeting.

"Come in," Summer said happily. "Hiya, Billy!"

"Hello, Summer. You all right?"

"Yeah, I'm peachy. I'm just worried about my friend here," she crooned, rubbing Angel's back warmly.

Angel looked around the living room. All the decorations had been removed and the place looked like a normal abode once again.

"Here's your video and hat." Summer picked them up off the couch and handed them to Angel.

"Thanks." Angel took them.

"Summer," Billy addressed her seriously, "You don't have

any idea who came to your party wearing that Scream get up?"

"No! But since Angel asked me about it, I did call a few friends. Only one of them recalls seeing someone standing around wearing it, but no one knew who it was."

"We found the mask," Angel informed her, "outside on the sissy bar of my bike."

"*Ew*, creepy!" Summer shivered in exaggeration. "Hey, detective, when are you going to get this weirdo?"

"Soon. Very soon," Billy replied bitterly.

"All right, sweetie," Angel began. "Let me go and I'll see you at the shop tomorrow morning."

"Okay. You sure you don't want to stay for a cup of coffee or something?" She followed them to her door.

"No, we're fine. I just want to call it a day." Angel tried to smile but he felt exhausted from all the stress.

"Okay, boss! See ya tomorrow."

Angel kissed her cheek, noticing Billy watching him as he did.

"Bye, detective!" She waved enthusiastically.

"Goodbye, Ms. Thompson." He smiled at her.

The two items in his hand, Angel walked to his bike and opened one of the saddlebags to stuff the hat and video inside. After he had clipped it closed, he found Billy standing beside him, a worried look on his face.

"So, I'll call you later?"

"You sure you're in any shape to ride?"

"Yeah. I'm fine."

"Call me when you get home. Can you do that? Just to let me know you got there all right?"

"Of course." Angel adored him, absolutely adored him.

Billy took a quick look around before he pecked Angel's lips. "You just go slow. No speeding."

"Yes, copper," Angel giggled.

"Where's your helmet?"

"Uh…" Angel lowered his head shyly.

"Oh no. You're not riding without a fucking helmet!" Billy roared.

"I'll be fine. Go. I'll call you." Angel straddled his bike and started it up. As the blast echoed around the quiet neighborhood, Angel took one last look at Billy's anxious expression, waved to him, and rode off.

Watching Angel glide away on that iron horse, Billy felt a sinking feeling in his stomach. If any harm came to Angel, he didn't know what he would do.

Chapter Eleven

Monday morning, Billy checked his workload, then drove off to Santa Monica High. He had already updated the report for Angel with each new incident that had taken place. With the escalation in activity, Billy was hoping he could convince the lieutenant and captain to give him a uniformed patrol unit to stand guard over Angel, but he knew he'd run into resistance. Personnel shortages. It was always the same story. If he couldn't get this solved quickly, he was going to take his vacation time and guard Angel himself.

His watch read nine thirty. Billy parked in a restricted zone in front of the school and climbed out, buttoning his suit jacket to cover his shoulder holster. His leather soles echoing in the empty hall, he found a sign directing him to the administrative offices and moved quickly down the linoleum floor before the bell rang and it flooded with teenagers.

Entering a waiting area with a secretary, Billy cleared his throat to get her attention as she typed away on a computer.

"Can I help you?" she asked.

Producing his police identification, Billy said, "Yes, my name is Detective Sharpe. I need some information about one of your students."

"Oh?" The woman appeared flustered. "Wait a moment. Can you have a seat?"

Though Billy nodded, he stood, looking at the plethora of posters about careers, drugs, sports, and library use. A moment later a smartly dressed gentleman emerged from an inner office.

"Detective?"

Billy took his outstretched hand.

"I'm Vice Principal Fiennes, what can I do for you?"

"I need some information on one of your students."

"Yes, can I ask what this is all about?"

Billy looked around the office first, then lowered his voice. "It's my belief that one of your boys is stalking Angel Loveday."

"Loveday? Oliver's father?"

"Yes."

"Do you know the boy's name?"

"Perry." As Billy said it, a look of complete comprehension passed over Mr. Fiennes' face. "I see that name rings a bell."

"Perry Brooks?" Mr. Fiennes confirmed. "Oh, yes. He's well known to me. Go take a seat in my office and I'll get his file."

"Thank you, sir." Billy walked to the room he was directed to and had a seat. Photos of a woman and three children were hanging on a wall along with certificates of awards and degrees.

Mr. Fiennes returned, closing his office door behind him. Billy watched as he sat down at his desk, setting the paperwork in front of him. "Here is his student file. It's usually confidential information, but I assume for police business it's accessible."

"I would just get a warrant from a judge, sir, so you are saving us both some time."

"Yes, of course. Here. Have a look through it and then ask me any questions you would like."

Nodding, Billy picked up the weighty folder, turning it to

face him so he could read it. He opened the cover. The first page had a photograph of the fiend. Billy tried not to cringe in disgust. Under his breath he muttered, "Typical."

"Sorry?"

"Nothing." Billy kept reading. Arson, harassment, drugs, truancy, property damage, the list kept going. Seeing Perry's home address, Billy took his pen and pad out of his pocket and copied it down. "Palos Verdes Estates? You know what his dad does for a living?"

"Investment banking. I've met both Perry's parents. His mother is a weak worrier and his father is too busy to bother with much of Perry's problems. Perry's an only child. I know he was in therapy for drug addiction, but I doubt his parents have kept up on it. They were pretty much in denial about it."

Billy wrote everything he needed as Mr. Fiennes spoke. Nothing he heard surprised him.

"This Loveday fellow. He was just here last week picking up his son Oliver after Oliver was involved in a fight."

"I've been doing the investigation on his case..." Billy was cautious about what he revealed. "...I did read in one of the reports that a flier that had been downloaded from the net was being circulated around this school. That's what led me here."

"Yes. That was unfortunate for Oliver's sake. So, Perry Brooks was the culprit? I should have known."

"Is he in class today?" Billy wanted to confront this creep so badly he ached.

"Let me check. He's rarely here. We tried to put a stop to his truancy, but again, without his parents to help us, it's useless. Hang on."

As Mr. Fiennes left the office, Billy turned back to the photograph again. From handling suspects for over twenty years, Billy knew the look of a sociopath. He was looking at photograph of one right now. These creatures had no conscience and were particularly nasty. Most ended up serial killers, arsonists, animal mutilators, and rapists. "Perry Brooks, you are one of the lowest life-forms on the planet," Billy hissed in disdain.

Hearing Mr. Fiennes returning, Billy stood up.

"As I expected. He's not here. I had the secretary call his home. His mother assumed he was in school because he wasn't home either."

"Right. Thanks for your help, Mr. Fiennes. It's been invaluable."

The vice principal shook his hand. "I hope you get the kid some help. He's on the road to a miserable future."

Behind bars, I hope. "Yes, well, we do our best to intervene and get kids back on the straight and narrow."

"I know. The police force is amazing around here. I admire everything you do."

"Thank you, sir. Good day." Billy waved at the secretary as he left, then found his way back out to where he'd parked his car. Just as he did, a bell rang and the noise of classes emptying out into the halls made its way out of the exit doors.

"Phew! Just in time." Billy shook his head, then climbed into his car and looked over his notes.

Angel thanked a customer who had just made a purchase. Smiling and watching him leave, he noticed Ray from the mystic shop next door coming in. Waving, Angel moved out from behind the counter to greet him. "Hey, Raymond. How's business?"

"Fine, Angel, just fine. How about you?"

"Great. What brings you in?"

"I just got a shipment of dragons in. I remembered how much your son Oliver liked them."

"Oh?" Angel perked up.

"Come and take a look. I want you to have first choice."

Nodding, Angel noticed Summer straightening a shelf nearby. "Summer? You mind if I go next door for a second?"

"Nope!"

"Be right back." Angel gestured for Ray to lead the way and followed him to the next shop. As they stepped in Angel could smell the incense and scented candles immediately. The tiny room was loaded with knickknacks and posters, board games and puzzles, crystal balls and tarot cards. Angel was brought to the window showcase. As he watched Ray removing an item from the display, Angel heard someone saying hello behind him. Spinning around he found Glynnis in her tie-dye smock and headband. Angel knew they were both ex-chemists and the whole earth-child look was an act, but the shop did well so he wasn't going to divulge their secret. "Hello, sweetie. How are you doing?" Angel smiled.

Glynnis hurried over to greet him. "I'm fine, Angel. Is Ray trying to sell you something?"

"He thought Oliver might like one of the new dragons that came in."

"Oh? Which one, Ray?" she shouted to her husband as he leaned gingerly into the glass window display.

Ray removed a modeled sculpture of a winged dragon with a small crystal globe under one if its claws. Handing it to Angel, Ray said, "What do you think?"

Nodding his head, Angel admired the detail but had second thoughts. "You know, Oliver hasn't really expressed too much interest in dragons lately. I'm not sure if he'll think it's too juvenile for him."

"You want to take it home to show him, then bring it back if he doesn't like it?" Ray offered.

"I think I'll let him decide. Why don't I bring him by Saturday? He can pick out one he likes."

"Sure, Angel. You want me to put this one aside?"

"I'll take my chances. Is it the only one you've got like

that?" Angel handed it delicately to Ray to put back into the window.

"I don't know…Glynnis? Can you check—"

"No," Angel stopped her. "Don't go to the trouble…let me bring Oliver here to take a look."

"You sure, Angel?" Glynnis asked. "I can check to see if we have another."

"No. It's okay. Let me get back to the shop. I don't like to leave Summer on her own."

"Okay." Glynnis stepped back to allow Angel to get by.

"Thanks, you two. You were great to think of Oliver. I appreciate it."

"No problem, Angel!" Ray waved.

Angel left and hurried to the bookshop.

Just as Ray was locking the glass case again, a strange young man entered the store. Ray looked back at Glynnis to see if she noticed him, but she had already gone to the back office to continue what she was doing before Angel had come in.

"Can I help you?" Ray asked, wanting to stand close to the door in case this pointy haired kid decided to snatch and run with something.

"Yeah…I want to see that dragon in the window."

Surprised at the request, Ray asked, "Which one?"

"The one with the ball under its hand."

Wondering about the odd coincidence, Ray opened the case and took out the same dragon he had just shown Angel. "You mean this one?"

"Yeah."

Ray watched warily as the odd pimple-faced kid took out a wad of cash and brought it to the cash register. After the weird kid paid for it, Ray wrapped it up back in its original box, and placed it in a bag. Immediately the kid left, not saying another word.

Once he had gone, Ray walked back to where Glynnis was sitting in the office. "A strange thing just happened."

"Oh?"

"A kid just came in and bought the same dragon I just showed Angel."

"Really? Crap, I better see if we have another one." She jumped to her feet and began checking the designs written on the outside of boxes.

Ray wandered back out to the storefront and looked outside. A strange sensation was making its way through him. It was too odd to be a coincidence.

Angel scribbled a list of groceries to pick up on the way home. As it neared closing time, Summer leaned against the doorway of the office so she could see both inside the office and out to the shop. "Going out tonight?"

"No. I don't think so. I just have to get some food. The cupboards are bare."

"You on the bike?"

"No. I got my car fixed. The damn battery went dead. I must have not closed the door all the way because the AAA guy said the door was ajar and the dome light drained the battery. You believe that?"

"Huh. Yeah, I guess. I lock my car so it's always closed tight."

"I thought I had, too. I guess I'm just distracted."

Summer pouted out her bottom lip, then sat down on the corner of Angel's desk. "I feel so bad that someone hurt you at my party. I can't believe someone I know would bring a creep like that."

"Don't worry about it." Angel looked up, asking, "Is the door locked?"

"Oops! No. Let me lock up."

"Please. Oh, and we need to get another door chime," Angel shouted as she raced to the front of the store.

Returning breathless from sprinting, Summer sat back on the corner of the desk and stared down at Angel as he added food items to his grocery list. "Yes. Door chimes. I have to remember that," she said.

"I can't even recall where I picked the last one up. It was there since we opened, years ago."

"I'll find one."

"Thanks." Angel set his pen down and folded his list, then caught Summer staring at him. "Yes?"

"That Detective Sharpe is one lucky guy."

Laughing shyly, Angel replied, "I'm the lucky one, Summer."

"At night, sometimes when I'm alone in bed? I picture the two of you—"

"Agh!" Angel held up his hand. "Too much information!"

"What?" She sighed. "Why is it okay for guys to imagine two women and not okay for a woman to imagine two guys?"

Standing up, putting his list into the pocket of his jeans, Angel shrugged. "I don't know, but it just is. Let's get the money out of the register and get out of here."

"Okay!" she exclaimed and raced back out of the office again.

Shaking his head at her innocence, Angel chuckled to himself in amusement. She returned with the cash drawer. Angel scooped up all the money, locked it up in the safe and then put his jacket on. As he did, Summer found her purse and sweater and got ready to leave. They walked to the front door together.

"You should buy some candy for Halloween. It's next weekend."

142

Angel exhaled tiredly. "Did we do it last year?"

"Yup. We had a bowl at the register."

"All right. I'll get one bag." He stepped outside, set the alarm, and locked the door.

After he jiggled the handle, they walked together to the parking area. Angel glanced into the mystic shop's window and was about to point out the dragon Ray had showed him to Summer. When he paused in front of the display, she asked what was wrong.

"It's gone. Huh. Maybe I should have bought it," Angel mused out loud.

"Something good in there?" She pressed her face to the window.

"No. Just a dragon sculpture. Ray thought Oliver would want it, but Oliver's not interested in dragons much anymore."

"Ask him about it when you get home."

"I thought I might bring him by on Saturday to take a look."

"Good idea."

Once they both were standing at their cars in the parking lot, Angel waved to Summer and then opened the door to his Camaro. Before he climbed in, he took a good look around the car and the area near the back of the shops. Nothing was unusual. Sitting behind the wheel, he started the car and drove off to the grocery store.

A minute later, a jeep followed him down the road.

At his desk in the property division office, Billy called Angel's home number and didn't leave a message when no one picked up. He tried the shop next and again received no answer. "I gotta get you a cell phone, Angel-baby," he vowed, then hung up and checked his watch.

He had another hour to kill at work, then he'd drive

directly to Angel's home, whether he heard from him or not.

Detective Jay Alexander passed Billy's desk, reading a report as he walked by. Billy paused to watch him when Jay caught his eye. As Billy waited curiously, Jay looked around the area first then closed the gap between them and leaned over Billy's desk. "Someone said you're still investigating that harassment case involving Loveday."

Billy sat up, bristling, ready for battle. "What about it?"

"You should have passed that one along to the crimes against persons unit, Bill. It don't look right."

"What the hell is that supposed to mean?"

"I mean," Jay hissed in warning, "that you look like you're defending a fucking queer."

In two seconds flat Billy had reached across his desk, grabbing Jay by the collar under his throat. Through clenched teeth, Billy snarled, "Watch yourself, Alexander. You wouldn't want the captain finding out you've said something politically incorrect. My guess is he'd have you suspended."

Jay glared down at Billy's hands, then shoved them off his shirt and stood back. "I get it," Jay asserted, "go ahead and have me suspended. It's better than the reputation you're getting."

As Jay walked away, Billy ground his jaw in fury.

Pushing a shopping cart around the mega food mart, Angel read his list of items and paused at the frozen food section. Opening one of the glass doors, he stuck his head inside the icy freezer to pick out some instant dinners for the nights he was too busy to cook for he and Oliver. A small stack of frozen dinners in his hands, he stepped back to place them in his cart and paused, looking around to make sure he had the correct basket. An enormous bouquet of flowers was filling the space over some food items. As a woman passed him by, he asked, "Excuse me. Did you put those in my basket by mistake?"

She looked down at the flowers and laughed, "No! I didn't.

They're beautiful though."

Angel picked up the mixture of roses and lilies and inspected underneath them. It was indeed his cart. He set the frozen dinners down and checked the area to make sure someone hadn't placed them in his by accident.

As he did, a card fell out, resting at his feet. The nice woman next to him picked it up and read it. "It says, 'Love you, Loveday'."

Angel shivered in terror.

"Are you Loveday? That is so sweet," the woman crooned. "I wish I had an admirer like that." She handed Angel the tiny card. "Lucky man!"

Once she walked away, Angel tried to breathe normally and checked the handwriting. A child's horrible scrawl. Grumbling under his breath, he wheeled his trolley back to the produce section, returned the flowers to their water bucket, then headed directly to check-out, shaking from the nerves.

Paying in cash, Angel tossed the tiny card into the trash, then pushed his cart to his car, all the while trying to look around him and not appear completely paranoid.

The moment he was seated in the driver's seat, he belted himself in, then sped out of the parking lot, checking his rear view mirror in fear that whoever this lunatic was he had it in for him big time.

Grinding to a stop on the gravel of his driveway, Angel looked at his dark house and knew Oliver was out again. Every night, no matter what day, Oliver was never home after school anymore. And not knowing where he was or who he was with was worrying Angel.

The grocery bags in his hand, Angel approached his door and stopped short. "Not again."

There, stuck to his door with another knife, was a photo. Setting the bags down, Angel took a closer look at the newest portrait. When he realized it was taken at Summer's party, he felt pale. "Oh, shit." He quickly opened his door and rushed in, grabbing the phone.

Billy was just heading out to his car when his mobile phone rang. Seeing it was Angel, he answered it quickly. "Hello, babe."

"Where are you at the moment?"

Hearing the fear in Angel's voice, Billy panicked. "I'm getting into my car. What the hell now?"

"Come to my place. Another knife in the door."

"For cryin' out loud!" Billy shouted. A fellow police officer noticed, staring at him. Climbing into his car, Billy warned, "Don't touch anything. I'm running code. Be there in a few."

"Code? Drive safe, Billy! I'm not in any danger!"

"Shut up. I'm on my way." Slipping the phone into his pocket, Billy screeched the tires out of the parking lot, set his blue and red flashing light on his dashboard, and flew westbound to Angel's home.

When Billy arrived he found Angel's door standing open. A nervous pang hit him in the stomach like a sledgehammer as he hurried to the gaping door. Seeing the knife and the picture still where Angel had said it would be, Billy began shouting for Angel in panic.

Angel hurried to the living room. "What's wrong?" Angel asked.

"Why the hell is the door standing open?" Billy pointed with his thumb over his shoulder.

"Oh. I was carrying in groceries. Jesus, Billy, how fast did you drive?"

"Never mind how fast." Billy walked back to the front door. Inspecting it closely, he knew exactly what it depicted without an explanation. Angel stood next to him, looking at it with him. "This is the night you were drugged at Summer's place."

"Yup."

"I hate this fucking pecker. If I ever get my hands on him—"

"Calm down." Angel rubbed Billy's back.

"Let me get some envelopes."

Angel nodded tacitly.

As he walked to the trunk of his car, Billy was muttering profanity under his breath. "Fucking, Perry-asshole-prick, if I ever catch up with you, you little SOB, I'll wring your pencil neck…"

"You talking to yourself, detective?" Angel shouted teasingly.

Knowing if he mentioned Perry again it would be discounted quickly, Billy kept his mouth shut on his suspicions for now. Bringing back two envelopes, wearing rubber gloves, he extricated the knife from the door, taking the incriminating photo down with it, bagged them separately, sticking them in his trunk. As he returned to where Angel had been standing, watching him, Billy snapped off his latex gloves and nudged Angel into the living room, closing the door behind him. "Look, Angel, no more leaving the damn door standing open. You shut it behind you. And you make sure before you open it to anyone you look outside first. You got it?"

"I got it," Angel replied, then added, "but I'm not a weakling, Billy. I can defend myself."

"Oh?" Billy took off his suit jacket revealing his holster. "Against one of these?" He gestured to his gun. Then making a point, Billy stormed to the kitchen, brought back a serrated blade and shouted, "Or how about against one of these?"

"All right," Angel chided quietly. "I get it."

Billy set the knife down on the kitchen counter, confronting Angel. "This guy, this suspect we're dealing with, he's a complete sociopath. He doesn't give a shit, Angel. They are the most dangerous kind of suspects to deal with. He's the type that will strangle the neck of a puppy. You get what I'm saying?"

Angel just stared at him blankly.

"He's going to escalate things. He already is," Billy warned. "This fucker is demented. He does drugs, he's already got a rap sheet a mile long."

"You know who it is!" Angel gasped.

Biting his lip, Billy didn't answer. "Ya got some hard booze?" He looked around the room.

"Billy!" Angel rushed him and grabbed his shirt collar. "Who the hell is it?"

"I don't know. Okay? I'm just giving you a profile. Scotch? Bourbon?"

"If he's got a rap sheet, why aren't his fingerprints on file?"

Billy thought to himself, *They are*. But he knew the prints that were lifted off the knife probably belonged to one of Perry' parents. Perry was too smart to leave evidence that obvious. "Booze?"

In a huff, Angel opened a cabinet and took out a bottle. He poured a large glass for Billy, handing it to him. Billy sniffed it. "Southern Comfort?"

"Yeah, sorry. I've got beer and wine, but this is left over from some birthday I celebrated ages ago."

Billy sipped it and winced. "It'll do." He sat down on the couch in a wide straddle and tried to relax. "Anything else happen that I should know about?"

Angel put the bottle of alcohol on the coffee table in front of Billy and said, "You mind if I get myself a beer first?"

"No, go ahead," Billy took another taste of the whiskey and grimaced at the after burn. "Your kid here?"

"No," Angel shouted back from the kitchen.

"Good," Billy mumbled quietly.

Once Angel returned, Billy patted the cushion on the couch next to him. "Now, sit down and talk to me, gorgeous."

Angel sat heavily and took a long drink of his cold beer. Wiping the foam off his lip, Angel then turned to face Billy on the couch. "I went grocery shopping on my way home. Someone put a large bouquet of flowers in my basket."

Billy ground his jaw in anticipation.

"I thought maybe someone had just made a mistake," Angel continued, "so I asked around, you know, if anyone had done it. No one had. And a card slipped out from them. It said, 'Love you, Loveday'."

Billy imagined he had steam shooting out his ears he was so enraged. "So, this moron was in the grocery store tailing you. I don't like this one bit, Angel. Not one bit!"

Angel set his beer down on the table and scooted closer, snuggling against Billy's chest.

Shooting back the nasty shot of alcohol quickly, Billy set his glass down as well, wrapping his arms around Angel and squeezing him tight. Leaning down, kissing Angel's hair, Billy knew he needed some hard evidence to get a search warrant of Perry's home. He just needed one break.

By eight o'clock they were naked and in bed. Angel sat up to listen, then whispered to Billy, "Oliver's home."

"So what? You want me to go?" Billy asked, smoothing his hand over Angel's arm.

"No. Let me just go out and see him." Kissing Billy's frown, Angel hopped out of bed and slid his jeans on, then threw the remote control at Billy and smiled. "Here. You can watch more of *Shame* if you want." Seeing that brightened Billy's expression, Angel winked at him and closed the bedroom door behind him. Oliver was already in the kitchen hunting for a meal.

"Hey, Oliver."

Standing up from behind the refrigerator door, Oliver said hello. "I'm starving."

"I just bought some frozen dinners if you want to stick one in the microwave."

"What did you eat?"

"Billy and I had some pasta."

"*He's* here?" Oliver sneered.

"Yes. He's in my room." Angel opened the freezer portion of the refrigerator and read off some of the selections. "How about chicken?"

"Okay." Oliver stepped back and allowed Angel to get by him.

"How was school?" Angel asked as he pulled the cardboard top off the meal.

"Okay." Oliver poured himself some pop and sipped it as he waited for his dinner, sitting down at the kitchen table.

"Do anything exciting after school?" Angel treaded lightly.

"Just hung out with Len. We jammed a little."

"Oh, cool. I liked what I saw of Len." Angel felt infinitely relieved.

"Yeah, he's all right. We wrote some songs, but it'll never amount to anything."

Once he had the dinner cooking, Angel faced his son, leaning back on the counter. "Why do you say that? You never know unless you try."

"I suppose." Oliver looked over in the direction of the bedrooms. "You just left that Bill-guy in there? Waiting for you?"

"Yes. Why? He's a big boy. He can stand being alone for a minute."

"Is he in your bed?"

"Oliver, don't start." Angel shook his head in warning.

"All right. I won't. I just think it's weird that you were gay for all that time and you never told me. It makes me feel like an idiot."

Exhaling, Angel sat down next to him at the table. "I was wrong. I was wrong to hide everything from you. I was just afraid that if I told you I'd get you upset, or it would screw you up somehow. I see now it was a mistake. I should have told you everything the minute you were old enough to understand. Please forgive me, Oliver. I can't do anything about it now."

After a long pause, Oliver met Angel's eyes. "It's okay, Dad."

Feeling euphoric at the comment, Angel reached for his son and embraced him. "Thank you, babe. I swear you're the best fucking son a dad could ever have."

"All right. Don't kiss me or anything."

Angel pulled back, smiling brightly at him. "Oh, Ray showed me a new dragon sculpture you might like. You still interested? It was pretty cool. It had a crystal orb on it."

"Nah. I think I've outgrown that stuff. But thanks for thinking about me." The microwave bell sounded. Oliver stood up and checked on his dinner. He removed a steaming dish and set it down to cool.

"No problem. Anything you need? We haven't been shopping in ages. You need some clothing?"

"No. I'm okay. Why don't you go back to your room? I feel bad keeping you from your boyfriend."

"I don't want you to eat alone."

"I'll watch TV."

"You sure?"

"Yeah. I want to catch the X-Files."

"Those old reruns still on?" Angel stood up when Oliver

did.

"I've never seen them. So they're not reruns to me."

"Okay, babe. Just knock if you need me."

"Thanks, Dad."

Smiling warmly to himself, Angel headed back to his room. When he opened his door he caught Billy with his legs spread, masturbating to the movie.

Closing the door behind him, Angel cracked up, "You are incorrigible!"

"I can't help it! Look at you!" Billy defended, pointing to the screen.

Tilting his head to see it, Angel found his image completely naked, being covered with suntan lotion by a two brawny lifeguards.

Covering his smile, Angel stared at Billy's imploring look. "All right, move over." Angel climbed on the bed and took over for Billy, cuddling up so he could share his pleasure when he climaxed.

Chapter Twelve

First thing in the morning, Oliver was standing at his locker in the hall of his high school. Shoving his backpack and jacket in it, he removed the notebook and textbook he needed for his class and slammed his locker closed. When he did, he realized Perry was standing right beside him, having been hidden from the open locker door. "Jesus, Per! Ya gave me a heart attack."

"Loveday…" Perry drawled.

Oliver took a moment to look at him, saying, "Man, are you stoned?"

"Loooveeedaaay…" Perry sang, laughing wickedly.

"What are you on, man?" Oliver took a step back from him.

"Why. Want some?"

"No thanks. Are you going to class like that?"

"Nah…hate school. It sucks."

Oliver glanced around the busy hallway. "You dropping out, Per?"

"Maybe. Who cares."

"You should care. You don't want to be stuck living at home your whole life."

"Ya sound like my old man. Shut up."

"Right. See ya." Oliver walked off, shaking his head. When he looked back, he found Perry inspecting something dark and metallic in his hand. Not wanting anything to do with him, or whatever object he might be secreting, Oliver raced to his first class.

Angel answered the phone in the shop while Summer helped a customer with a travel book. "Uncut Buzzard, can I help you?"

"Hello, gorgeous."

"Hey," Angel replied, softening his tone to one of completely lovesickness. "Whatcha doin', baby?"

"Look, since I can't get an okay from the captain on an extra patrol unit for you, I've requested some time off. I want to just hang around for a few days to make sure nothing happens to you."

"You don't have to do that, Billy. I swear you make me feel like an invalid." Angel walked with the cordless phone to his back office where he could speak privately.

"I'm not doing that. Angel, listen to me. You're a big, physically fit man. I'm not in any way trying to emasculate you. Okay? I just love you and I'm scared shitless this moron is going to hurt you."

Angel blinked his eyes. "You...you love me?" He felt his stomach flutter.

After a pause, Billy asked sheepishly, "Did I say that?"

"You did!" Angel laughed in delight.

"I'm not good at that fuzzy stuff, Angel."

"You don't have to be." Angel couldn't believe how excited it made him. "If..." Angel stammered, "...if I say it, will you think I'm some immature twit?"

Billy burst out laughing. "Hell no! Say it!"

Angel looked around the outside area of his office quickly,

then cupped the phone and whispered, "I love you, Detective Sharpe, you fantastic stud, you."

A long deep breath came over the line as Angel imagined Billy to be savoring the comment. Finally waiting long enough, Angel asked impishly, "Well?"

"I'm at work, babe."

"Oh, come on," Angel teased.

Another pause followed, then Angel heard very softly, "I love you."

Instantly his face heated up from the thrill. "Oh, Christ, Billy, you are so incredible. I am so lucky I found you."

"Ditto, gorgeous. Now, back to what I was saying. Look, I've put in a request for some vacation time. I'm not going to be a pest. I'm just going to linger on the periphery. Okay? You won't even notice me."

"Yeah, right. Until you push me over my desk and screw me."

"All right, until then. Let me get back to work. Call me later."

"I will, Billy."

"And please, Angel. Watch yourself."

"Don't worry." Angel hung up and brought the phone back to the front counter where Summer was ringing up a sale. He replaced the receiver on the cradle and gave her some space to complete the transaction, walking to the shelves to straighten them up.

Sensing her standing behind him, Angel looked over his shoulder at her.

She grinned, saying, "You just talked to Billy."

"How can you tell?" he humored her.

"You're glowing!"

Feeling a cross between a silly little teenager and man in love, he didn't answer, just smiled to himself.

By four-thirty Angel was home and checking the cottage for any sign of Oliver. Shaking his head in annoyance, Angel was about to call Billy to see what he was doing after work, when the phone rang.

He picked it up and said hello.

"Ah...Loveday?"

"Yes. Who's this?"

"Ah...it's Perry. Look, Oliver's in real trouble..."

Angel felt sick. "Trouble? What kind of trouble?"

In a slow slurring voice, Perry replied, "He got beat up after school. He's a real mess."

"Oh, shit. Are you with him? Where is he?" Angel grabbed his car keys.

"Uh...he's here with me."

"Where?" Angel shouted as he approached his front door. "Where is he?"

"At my house."

"What's your address, Perry?" Angel scrambled for a pen and paper.

Perry rattled it off slowly. "Come quick. He's real bad."

"Shit. I'm on my way." Angel threw the phone down and raced out of the door.

Oliver stood behind Len as he sat at the computer in Len's bedroom. Len said, "Check this out, Oliver."

Leaning over Len's shoulder, Oliver watched as a video downloaded from MySpace. In a few seconds he watched Perry trying to rap a song he had obviously written. The minute he heard a part of it, Oliver burst out laughing with Len.

Len tried to speak through his hysterical laughter, "What an idiot. You believe he put this on MySpace where everyone on the planet can see it?"

"What the hell is he saying?" Oliver tried to control his giggling fits.

Len reloaded it and hit the play button again.

"...*the king...he is the king of my dreams, king of inseams, no one compares, no one splits hairs...*"

Oliver doubled over in laughter, holding his belly he was roaring so loudly. Len wiped his eyes as they teared up, trying to listen to the ridiculous lyrics.

"Oh, man, he is so screwed up," Oliver choked between laughter.

"No kidding." Len deleted the screen. "What a freak."

Billy checked the time. Picking up the phone on his desk, he called Angel's home number. When his machine picked up he left a message. "Hey, babe. It's me. I'll be on my way in about forty-five minutes. So, see you at your place." Hanging up, he swiveled his chair back to the computer and finished typing up the report he had started.

Angel struggled at first with the address. He knew if he continued traveling south on Highway 1 he'd eventually hit the estates. Though he'd never driven through that area, he knew of it, and of the wealth of the property.

Slowing down as he came upon the correct street, Angel felt so sick for Oliver he could hardly think straight. Finally the house number appeared on a golden colored brick wall. Pulling into the driveway, Angel shut off his engine and hurried out of his car to the imposing mansion's front door. Ringing the bell, then banging on the door, he grew impatient when no one answered. Impulsively he tried the door handle. When it opened, he pushed back the enormous door and shouted out, "Hello? Perry? Oliver?" Entering the grand foyer with a hanging crystal chandelier, Angel listened for a noise of habitation and heard nothing. "Hello?" Looking around the ground floor quickly, Angel grew frustrated and boldly dashed up the curling staircase, taking two stairs at a time. All the while he was shouting for Oliver or Perry in vain.

Along a lengthy narrow corridor, Angel kept poking his head into each imposing bedroom, calling out their names. At the end of the hallway, to the left, was a door. Angel knocked, opening it. "Perry? Oliver?"

Pushing it back, Angel stepped inside an oddly shaped space. It seemed too small for a bedroom and veered sharply to the right creating an angle he couldn't see beyond. Pausing, looking at one wall curiously, he suddenly noticed it was completely papered with cut-outs and photographs. When he drew nearer, he realized those images where of him.

"What the?" He stepped closer, squinting his eyes in disbelief.

There, on a wall that spanned more than fifteen feet in length, was every photograph and advertisement he had ever posed for. Some were duplicates with different captions attached to them. A few he recognized instantly from the ones that had been left in the shop, around Redondo, and his home. It was mesmerizing. Walking slowly down the length of wall, Angel read the eerie titles, some familiar, others not; *Prince of Porn, Scepter of the gods, Nude Dude, Father Fornicator…*

"Jesus," he mumbled, moving along the collage slowly, inspecting each item. Articles that had been found in archive newspapers appeared, some so obscure he himself had never seen them. Enlargements of the covers of his videos were displayed in a mosaic pattern; at least a dozen of them were in a design, slightly overlapping, as if it were an advertisement created by Plimpton's movie house. Next came a mixture of photographs from a Polaroid camera, a digital camera, and a 35 mm with a zoom lens. In them he was getting into his car, sitting on his bike, walking on the beach with Billy, in his bedroom dressing, through the window of his shop helping customers. Under that montage of real snapshots was a dragon sculpture. Angel was so bewildered by the quantity of images he didn't even realize where he had seen it before. Moving on, staring at the bizarre wall in this macabre museum-like gallery, Angel found a small-screen television. On it was a short video of when he was trapped on the beach. Replaying over and over was the short clip of him standing at the bottom of the sandy cliff, staring up, asking for help. Over and over.

"What the fuck?" Angel had almost forgotten why he had come. Never in his life, even including all the attention from his manic fans, had he ever seen anything quite as demented as this exhibition. When he came to the end of the wall, there on the last section was a collection of photos of his cock. In every different pose from his past where he had been exposed, that one piece of his genitalia had been cropped and blown-up to fill a page. The sight of it sickened him so badly he felt weak in the knees. "For cryin' out loud," Angel moaned. Then, pausing, his heart a deafening rumble in his ears, Angel thought he heard something. Turning around slowly, he imagined he was in a movie, and it was at this point that the audience began shouting for the hero to get the hell out of the house.

Finding his courage, Angel spun one hundred and eighty degrees to look behind him. "Oh, crap," he groaned.

Billy packed up his paperwork, shut off his computer, and checked his watch. As he walked out to his car he dialed Angel again from his mobile phone. When the answering machine picked up, Billy grumbled, "Where are you? I'm on my way." He hung up and got into his car, driving to Angel's cottage by the sea.

Swallowing down his fear, Angel looked into Perry's bloodshot eyes. "What do you want, Perry?" Sitting still as a corpse, Perry was posed as if he were some mad dictator waiting for James Bond to be brought before him for torture.

Distracted by Perry's watery eyes and red, waxy skin, Angel didn't notice what he was holding until he forced himself to look down at Perry's lap. Seeing the gun there in Perry's hand almost made Angel cry. "No. Don't. Perry, why are you doing this?"

Billy pulled into Angel's driveway and didn't see his Camaro. Trying not to get worried, knowing he had some car trouble earlier that week, he climbed out of his unmarked sedan and knocked on the door. No one answered. Instantly Billy jumped the side fence, calling Angel's name and looking through the windows for him. The back door was locked. "Shit, shit, shit!" Billy clenched his teeth.

Scanning the beach first, Billy had a sinking feeling that something was terribly wrong. Making his way back to the front of the cottage, climbing over the fence again, he took out his mobile phone and called Summer.

"Hello?"

"Summer? It's Billy. Look, did Angel say he was doing anything after work? You know, like shopping or an errand?"

"No. He went grocery shopping yesterday, I think? Or was that Saturday? I'm not sure."

"Nothing today? He didn't say he was doing anything today?" Billy began to pace.

"No. Why? What's happened? Oh, no, Billy, is something wrong?"

"He's not home. I'm standing in front of his house and he's not home."

"He must have just had an errand. That's it. Maybe he had to pick up Oliver."

"Maybe." Billy didn't think so. "Okay, if you hear from him, call my cell phone, will ya? You need the number or do you have caller ID?"

"Nope, I got it."

"Good. See ya, Summer." Billy hung up and shifted his weight side to side, trying to decide what to do.

Angel backed up slowly until he was leaning against the desk that was in front of the wall of pictures. "Perry, why are you doing this?"

Perry didn't answer, just stared with glazed eyes.

"Is Oliver here?" Angel tried to keep his voice calm. "You said Oliver was in trouble. Is he here?"

"Loveday..."

"What? Perry, when are your parents coming home?"

"Loveday..."

"*What*? Perry, put the gun down. Will ya? Just put the damn gun down."

"Everyone had you..." Perry slurred, as if his tongue were thick.

"Had me? Had me what?" Angel wondered if he ran away if Perry would shoot him in the back. "Had sex with me?"

"Had you, had you, had you..."

"Christ, Perry, what the hell are you on?" Angel glimpsed towards the door again.

"Had Loveday's cock...his long hard cock."

"Come on, Perry, you're too young to be saying shit like that." When Perry adjusted his hand on the gun, Angel jolted in fear. "Can you put that thing down so we can talk?" Perry didn't. He just adjusted his finger on the trigger.

"So..." Angel figured if he kept babbling sooner or later someone had to come home and save him. "...you...you want sex? Is that what this is all about?"

"Had you, had you, had you..."

Billy was about to explode, feeling useless waiting for

Angel to come home when he could be in big trouble. Checking the time again, he was about to start the car and go looking for him when a pick-up truck pulled up and Oliver jumped out.

Billy quickly exited his car and approached him as the truck drove off.

"Oliver, where's your dad?"

"Huh? I don't know. Isn't he home?" Oliver looked around the driveway.

"Open the door," Billy instructed.

Nodding, Oliver opened his front door and pushed it back for Billy to enter. Billy looked through the small cottage quickly. Nothing seemed out of place.

"Does he usually leave you a note, Oliver?"

"Sometimes. Let me check my messages." Oliver set his school bag down and hit the button on the answering machine. Only the ones Billy left played for them.

"Shit." Billy began to wring his hands nervously.

"What's wrong?" Oliver asked. "Is Dad okay? Do you know where he is?"

Snapping, Billy shouted, "No, I don't know where he fucking is! Why do you think I'm asking you?"

"All right, don't bite my head off. He's okay. He probably just went to the store or something." Oliver sat down on the sofa.

"I'll give him ten more minutes, then I'm calling patrol out."

Oliver shrugged, checking his watch.

It was nearing six and Billy was growing frantic.

"Is that what this is all about, Perry? Sex?" Angel tried to clarify, but Perry didn't respond. "Man, Perry, whatever your ingesting it's fucking you up. You on crack?"

"Everyone had you...had you..."

162

"Stop saying that," Angel cringed. "Not that many people had me, if it's in the way you're implying. What's the deal with the photos, Perry?" Angel pointed to the wall behind him. "Does your mom and dad know about that horrible wall of shit?"

Perry moved the gun again, raising it up towards Angel's chest. Angel put his hands up in defense. "Okay. Calm down. Okay? Tell me what you want."

"I can't have you...have you...have you..."

"No. No, Perry, you can't. For too many reasons to list. But that doesn't mean we can't talk to each other. You need me as a friend? I can be that."

"Have you...have your cock...your cock..."

"Perry. Don't talk like that. Look, can you put the damn gun down? I'm having a hard time concentrating with that thing pointing at me. I won't go anywhere, all right?"

"You got a big dick, Loveday."

"So I've heard. Can I take that gun?" Angel put out his hand. "Can I take that gun just to put it aside, Perry?"

It elevated to Angel's face. Angel backed down and lowered his hand. "So? How do we resolve this, Perry? Huh? You kill me? Is that your plan? Kill the nasty porn star?"

"Nasty porn star," Perry laughed in amusement. "Kill the nasty porn star."

"I didn't say it to give you the idea. No one has to die, Perry. Look, let's go out somewhere. Okay? You want to walk on the beach and talk? Maybe we can get you some help—" When the look on Perry's face changed to rage, Angel shut up.

"That's it," Billy shouted as he stood. "He's in trouble. I'm not sitting here anymore." Billy stormed to the door. Before he left he shouted to Oliver, "You got my mobile phone number, kid. If he calls you call me right away, you got it?"

"Yeah," Oliver replied nervously. He walked to the door behind Billy and said, "You think he's all right, don't you?"

"I don't know. But I'm going to find him." Billy headed to his car and started the engine. He had only one hunch, but it was the best one he had.

Angel kept perfectly still and quiet. The low murmur of that replaying video tape finally stopped. The house was dead calm. Angel was praying Perry's parents would come home. It had to be nearing six. He just didn't want to make a move to peek at his watch.

In the eerie stand-off silence, Angel got a better look at this troubled teen. The drug use had already taken its toll. Perry's skin was gray with blotchy red patches. His fingers were dirty and stained. Angel knew that was most likely from smoking out of a crack pipe. Flashing back to his own youth, Angel remembered doing his own chemical concoctions. For five years he had stayed perpetually stoned. Every night the cast would get together to drink themselves into oblivion or snort coke, take pills, smoke pot, anything to get off. Is that what he looked like back then?

"Perry…" Angel began again slowly. "I was there. I was into drugs big time. I know what you're going through."

"Shut up."

Angel bit his lip. Obviously this wasn't the way to escape with his life. "What do you want me to do, Perry?"

A snickering smirk made it to Perry's ugly face.

Angel was sorry he asked. "Look, just let me go. Let's call it a day, can we just call it a day, Perry?"

That pudgy hand adjusted its grip on the pistol again.

"Fine!" Angel shouted in frustration. "You want to see my dick? Is that what it's about? I show you it and you let me go home?"

"Scepter of the gods…prince of porn…"

164

"Yeah, yeah, I know. You think you're the first one to give me a hard time over that era in my life? I got news for you, you aren't."

"Had you...had you...they all had you..."

"You already said that." Angel was sick to death of this game. "Look, if you're going to kill me, kill me. What's with the damn delay?"

Perry sat up slowly, moving his second hand to steady the gun. Angel knew he never should have called his bluff. Flinching back, Angel shouted, "I didn't mean it! Okay? I don't want to die, Perry. Stop. Put it down. Okay?"

When Billy pulled into the long paved driveway and spotted Angel's car, he felt instant relief. Then, realizing what was going on, he shut off the engine and raced out of the car to the front door.

"Perry...please. I'm begging you. Point that thing somewhere else!"

"I couldn't have you."

"Yes, you can. Okay? What do you want? You want sex? You want to suck me? Tell me." Angel made as if he were opening his pants.

"They all had you...had you..."

"Jesus, Perry! I'm giving it to you on a silver platter. Okay? You want my dick?" Angel stopped just short of exposing himself and waited to see if that made any difference.

"Oliver had you...had you all his life."

"He's my son, Perry," Angel chided. "I'm his father."

"All your life...I had nothing. I had nothing all my life."

"Right. Now we're getting somewhere. Talk to me." Angel folded his arms over his chest. "Tell me about it."

When Perry stood up off the chair, teetering unsteadily,

Angel gasped and tried to step back. "What are you doing? Perry? Don't do it, whatever it is. Please. It may be a nasty little life, but it's the only one I've got."

Billy found the front door ajar. Pushing it back so he could see inside, he removed his gun from his holster and went room to room on the bottom floor quietly, looking around.

"Kneel, Loveday."

"Perry, come on. Not like this." Angel shivered as he imagined being executed mob style.

"Kneel!"

Angel lowered down slowly to his knees. Suddenly it wasn't a game any longer and he felt like crying he was so terrified.

Perry held the gun in his right hand and fumbled with his trousers with his left. As Angel watched he cringed, revolted at the idea of that thing coming anywhere near him. But it was becoming obvious what Perry wanted.

Billy cleared the bottom floor and began ascending the stairs. Keeping alert for any sound, when he got to the top landing, he paused, listening. Not a whisper met his ears, and he was beginning to wonder if Perry hadn't taken Angel somewhere else to torment.

Angel winced as a tiny, limp, pudgy penis was exposed from a pair of army fatigue shorts. Perry's pale, furry legs were fat at the calves and ankles, his tennis shoes were filthy and worn out. Angel peered up hesitantly. The gun barrel was right in front of his face and a shaking fat, white hand with dirty, bitten nails gripped the handle like iron.

"Suck it, Loveday."

Angel swallowed down some black water at the thought. *Here it is, all those years of making slutty movies has finally caught up to you. Now it's your time to pay. Pay for all the embarrassment you caused your family, your father, your son...*

A revolting smell reached his nose as Perry leaned closer. Unable to prevent it, Angel began sobbing. "No, Perry...please."

Room after room, Billy cleared them for occupants. One room was left. At the end of the hall there was a door standing open and a light emitting from it. Moving silently, his weapon in his hand, Billy stood at the doorway and peeked in.

Angel felt a nudge. The gun was poking his head. Tears running down his face, Angel began reaching forward, sick to his stomach to the point where he felt if he put that thing in his mouth he would vomit.

Suddenly an authoritative voice ordered, "Drop the gun! NOW!"

Angel froze and prayed Billy had a good shot over his head.

Seeing that freak forcing his lover to perform a sex act on him, Billy almost shot first and asked questions later. But being an expert marksman and an honest cop, he gave the kid one chance.

That set of blood red eyes darted up to Billy's, matching his rage. Billy knew this punk kid saw he meant business. "NOW!" Billy steadied his aim, had a clear shot over Angel's head and readied his stance to shoot.

At the gun blast Angel flinched and shouted out in fear not knowing if he was hit. A second blast sounded. Finally Perry dropped in front of him with two holes in his forehead. Angel stood up and sprinted back to where Billy was standing. Billy never took his eyes off of Perry. Moving Angel behind him, Billy walked warily over to where Perry was lying. Slowly, Billy took the cell phone from his jacket pocket and dialed. "Yeah, 911? It's Detective Sharpe here from the Santa Monica Police Department. I need an ambulance, a marked unit, and a supervisor to the following location…"

Angel was shaking so badly his teeth were chattering. When Billy had finished with his phone call, Angel asked, "Is he dead?"

"Yeah. I'm too good a shot. I just needed to call the ambulance as protocol." Putting his gun back into his holster, Billy then looked up at the wall of paper. "Mother fucker. Look at this."

Angel still felt ill, but approached Billy to lean against him as he inspected the collage. "I can't believe he did this," Angel moaned.

"I'm telling ya, Angel, this type of suspect is a real wacko. There's no reasoning with him."

"I know. I tried. How did you know to come here?" Angel asked.

"A hunch. Though you didn't believe me, I knew it was this creep. I went to the school and the file they had on him made it pretty fricken obvious."

They both heard a noise. Billy left the room and hurried to the hall. Angel followed him quickly. When they looked over the rail of the second floor, a man and a woman were standing in the foyer, looking up.

"Who the hell are you? What are you doing in my house?" the heavyset man in the three-piece suit asked.

Billy looked back at Angel first with a pained expression, then descended the stairs. He produced his police identification, saying, "Are you Mr. and Mrs. Brooks?"

Angel walked down the stairs slowly to listen.

"Yes. Where's Perry? Why are you in my house?"

The timid middle-aged woman covered her mouth and asked, "Did something happen to our Perry?"

The next sound they heard was the wailing of a siren.

Billy knew what he had to tell Perry's parents wasn't going to be easy. Before he got his chance, a medic crew, two uniformed officers, and a sergeant came flying into the house.

Mr. Brooks stopped everyone from proceeding and began shouting for someone to explain it to him while Mrs. Brooks covered her mouth and whimpered.

Billy shouted to Mr. Brooks, "Hang on, okay? Let me get the medics upstairs. I'll tell ya what's going on in a minute. Hang on!" He held out his hand but knew Mr. Brooks needed to know. He addressed the ambulance crew, "Upstairs. That man up there will show you to the correct room." Billy waved to Angel who waved back in acknowledgement. The two men raced up to Angel with their kits.

"Now, let me talk to the sergeant, all right?" Billy nodded to the supervisor and pulled him aside. "Look, I shot an armed suspect upstairs. He's dead. He was threatening to kill Angel Loveday, the man who was just standing on that landing. The suspect's name was Perry Brooks. He was seventeen. These are his parents and they have no idea what's going on."

The look on the sergeant's face told Billy he couldn't believe what he was hearing. Billy asked, "What do you want me to do first? Show you the body? Or explain to his parents what's going on?"

"Show me the body."

"Right." Billy pointed at the two uniformed cops, ordering them, "You two, stay with Mr. and Mrs. Brooks. Don't let them go upstairs. Guard the staircase for the follow-up unit." The cops nodded.

Mr. Brooks went mad, shouting, "What is the meaning of

this? I demand to know what's going on! If this has anything to do with my son, I want to know now! I'll have your badges! You hear me?"

As Billy led the sergeant up the stairs, he mumbled, "Yeah, yeah, take my fucking badge..." He heard the sergeant laughing softly behind him.

They met the medics coming back towards them down the hall.

Billy stopped to talk to them. "I knew he was dead. Sorry, boys. It was just to cover my ass."

"No problem." They handed him a piece of paper with their findings.

Billy took the paper and asked, "Did you touch the gun?"

"No, sir." They shook their heads and left.

When Billy looked up, Angel was standing there looking forlorn, his arms crossed tightly over his chest in defense. Billy wanted to comfort him, but he had to get back to business first.

"This way, sergeant." Billy passed Angel and directed the supervisor to the correct room. Gesturing for the sergeant to enter, Billy waited as he took in the contents of the room, including the wall.

"How long was he stalking the victim?" the sergeant asked as he moved towards the body.

Billy looked back at Angel and asked, "Two weeks?"

Angel nodded silently.

"About two weeks," Billy confirmed, then watched as the sergeant investigated the position of Perry's body and the gun still clamped in his dead hand.

"Fuck ugly kid," the sergeant mumbled.

Billy chuckled to himself.

Taking out his mobile phone, the sergeant dialed and then said, "Homicide? This is Sergeant Wilson. Look, I need you boys out here. I've got an officer involved shooting, suspect

DOA, and victim here at the scene."

As Sergeant Wilson gave his investigations unit more details, Billy looked back at Angel. There, standing in the doorway, lost, was the lovely star of the Eighties Plimpton films. Unable to resist, and feeling as if he had the time to spare now, Billy reached out for Angel, drew him into a warm embrace and squeezed him tight, rocking him. "You're all right, now. It's over."

"I still don't know what happened to Oliver."

"Oh. He's fine. He's home. Here." Billy gave Angel his cell phone. "Call him."

"He's home?" Angel asked in disbelief.

"Yeah. I told him to sit tight."

Anxiously, Angel dialed his home number and stood out in the hall.

Billy looked back at the sergeant who had obviously spied the embrace. "Homicide is en route. We'll need your gun. You want to call your captain?"

"Yeah," Billy sighed tiredly. "He ain't gonna be thrilled."

"No, captains rarely are when their cops are involved in a fatal shooting." Sergeant Wilson then whispered, "You want me to tell the parents?"

"Nah, I'll do it. You just back me when they go ballistic."

"Got it," he replied and patted Billy's arm.

"Oliver?"

"Dad! Where are you? Billy was here, and we couldn't figure out where you were."

Angel watched as Billy and Sergeant Wilson walked down the hall together. So he could speak privately, Angel was standing outside in the hall by the room where Perry was lying. "I know. Look, it's a long story, but Perry called me at around four thirty. He said you were involved in another fight and were hurt."

"Perry called you?"

"Yes. He told me you were with him. I'm at his house in Palos Verdes right now."

"What? I don't get it."

"Oliver, it was Perry who had been stalking me."

"No way!"

"Yes way. Listen to me. I don't have much time." Angel could hear Mr. Brooks screaming profanity and threatening the police. "I came here looking for you. When I got here, Perry had a gun and pointed it at me."

"I don't believe this."

"Me neither. Well, to make a long story short, Billy showed up, shot Perry before he could kill me, and now Perry is dead. I suppose it'll be a while before I can get home. I probably need to write statements for the police." No reply returned. "Oliver?"

Oliver cried, "I'm so sorry, Dad. I never should have brought that creep over. I am so sorry."

"Stop. It's not your fault."

"Are you okay? Did he hurt you?"

"I'm fine." Angel heard Billy shouting for him. "I have to go. You just don't worry. I'll be home later. Okay?" Angel heard his shaky goodbye and hung up. Inhaling deeply, he walked down the hall and descended the stairs to the waiting crowd. Homicide had arrived and the foyer was jammed with officials.

Angel watched Billy handing his gun to someone in uniform. Several high-ranking supervisors with gold stripes on their collars and shoulders were there, asking questions. As he made his way down to the bottom of the steps, he heard one of the cops mention, "The press is outside."

Angel cringed. He had kept hidden for almost twenty

years. Visions of his old photographs being printed on front pages of newspapers haunted him like a poltergeist.

Billy's voice was going. He was becoming hoarse from all the explaining he had to do. Why was he investigating a crime off duty? Why didn't he call a uniformed officer to the scene? Was the shooting necessary? Did he break into the home? Did the victim break in?

Rubbing his face in agony at the mound of paperwork to come, Billy looked up from the many queries to see his lover appearing as drained as he felt. Ignoring the noise momentarily, Billy crossed the white tiled floor to where Angel stood. Pushing Angel's long straight hair back from his face, Billy asked, "How are you holding up?"

"I'm all right."

"Did you talk to Oliver?"

"Yes." Angel returned Billy's cell phone, handing it to him.

Billy slipped it into his pocket, then he put his arm around Angel's shoulder and brought him over to his captain. "Sir? This is Angel Loveday. The victim who was being stalked, and he's..." Billy took a big swallow for courage, "...he's my lover. The suspect had a gun to his head at the time and was forcing him to perform a sexual act. When I ordered the suspect to put down the gun he refused. I gave two verbal warnings, then I fired. I was afraid for Angel's life."

"Okay. That's fine. Just come down to headquarters and write a statement. I'll need one from you as well, Mr. Loveday."

"Yes, sir." Angel nodded.

Billy whispered into Angel's ear, "Give me your car keys. I'll have one of the uniforms drive your car home for you."

Angel reached into his pocket for them. Billy called over one of the young cops and instructed him on the detail. The cop nodded and tapped his partner to help him out.

"Okay." Billy reached for Angel's hand. "Come on, I'll drive us to the precinct."

Just as Angel was leaving with Billy, Mr. Brooks came charging back into the foyer, shouting, "You expect me to believe my Perry was stalking that porn star? That's preposterous! My Perry was a good boy. An A-student! That man is the pervert! He's twisted it all around! He's a pedophile who was after my teenage boy! Arrest him! You can't let him go. I'll sue all of you! You hear me? I'll see all of you in court for murdering my little boy!"

Behind him Mrs. Brooks was wailing.

Billy was about to roar something defensive in reply when he noticed Angel's lip quivering and his eyes filling with tears. "Come on, baby. Let's get you out of here."

Leaving the string of accusations behind, Billy brought Angel to his sedan and opened the passenger door for him. After he was inside, Billy closed the door and walked around the car to the driver's side. Before he started the engine he twisted in his seat to face Angel. "Ignore that ignorant bastard. He don't know what the hell he's talking about."

"I just know what I would feel like if anything happened to Oliver."

"Don't even compare Oliver to that sociopath." Billy looked out of his windshield and watched as more units responded to handle the growing crowd of press and spectators. "Let's get the fuck out of here before one of these vultures figures out who you are." Billy started the car, put his blue and red light on again, and slipped out of the mob quickly.

When he was on the road, he reached out to hold Angel's hand, kissing his knuckles. "One last hurdle of paperwork, and we're home free, babe. Hang in there."

"I will. Don't worry about me. I'm just sick about what you have to go through at work because of me."

"Because of you?" Billy choked. "Because of that freak of a punk Perry. Don't even think of taking any of the blame. He had you on your fucking knees in front of him with a gun to your head!"

"Stop."

Billy bit his lip and tried to calm himself down. For Angel's sake, he had to calm down.

By midnight Billy drove Angel back to the cottage. The Camaro was parked out front and the home was lit from within. Once Angel exited the car, Billy wrapped his arm around Angel's waist and held him tight as they walked to the front door. Using his key, Angel opened the door and looked around for his son.

Whispering, Billy said, "He must be in bed, Angel."

"Let me just check." Waiting for Billy's nod in understanding, Angel then tiptoed to Oliver's bedroom and opened the door. Seeing him safe and sound was a huge relief to Angel.

"Dad?" Oliver opened his eyes groggily.

"Hey, baby. You okay?"

"What happened? Did you have to go to the police station?"

Angel sat down next to Oliver on the bed and rubbed his arm through the sheets. "Yes. I had to write all sorts of statements down about everything that had happened to me since the first day when the video showed up at the bookshop."

"I still can't believe Perry was stalking you and now he's dead."

"I know. It's crazy."

"You want me to take tomorrow off from school? You know, to hang around with you?"

Angel smiled sweetly. "That's not necessary unless you

feel you want a day off. I was planning on going into work."

"You were?"

"Yes. I'm fine, Oliver. Now that Perry is gone, I don't have to worry anymore."

"Huh. I guess so."

"Go back to sleep. I'll talk to you more about it in the morning."

"Is Billy here?"

"Yes," Angel replied hesitantly.

"Good."

"Good?" Angel asked in surprise.

"Yeah. When he's around, I know you'll be all right. He really likes you, Dad."

"I know. Thanks for being so cool about him."

"It's okay. Goodnight, Dad. I'm glad you're all right."

"Me, too. Goodnight, son." Angel kissed his cheek before he left the room. He looked around for Billy. Poking his head into his bedroom, he found a naked detective sitting up against the headboard, sipping a glass of whiskey. A cold beer was on the nightstand, waiting for someone to drink it.

Smiling tiredly, Angel closed the bedroom door and started taking off his clothing. "That beer for me?"

"It is." Billy smiled.

After he tossed off the last piece of his clothing, Angel crawled into bed and reached for the brew. Billy handed it to him carefully, then they tapped glasses in a toast.

"To peace and quiet?" Angel offered.

"To peace, quiet, and a long romantic relationship," Billy countered.

"You ol' softy," Angel teased.

"You got me in an unguarded mood. It doesn't happen often, but damn, I'm so exhausted I'll say anything."

"Oh? You get punchy when you're tired?" Angel took a long swallow of his beer, then rested it on the nightstand.

"Yeah. What can I say?"

"Nothing. I love it. So? Get mushy with me, lover. Tell me something now that you would be reluctant to tell me when you're feeling alert and tough."

Billy laughed softly, averting his eyes.

"Oh? Gone shy on me suddenly?" Angel smiled wryly.

"All right. You want me to tell you something that I'll deny I ever told you if you blackmail me?"

Tilting his head at the odd disclaimer, Angel said, "Uh, yes…I think."

"Fine." Billy finished his shot of booze, placing the glass aside, then rolled over, propped his head up in his hand and replied, "I've loved you since I was eighteen. But, the man I loved then was a two-dimensional poster of a sex god. The love I feel for you now is deep, rich, and satisfying. You mean everything to me, Gabriel Loveday. Everything."

Angel blinked his eyes in awe. "Wow."

"There. That's my midnight, I'm exhausted, confession. Now I need to sleep."

After Billy reached up to turn off the light, Angel curled up on his chest and whispered, "And you are the man of my dreams, Detective Sharpe."

"Go to bed, Loveday."

"Goodnight, Billy."

Chapter Thirteen

Angel heard Oliver's alarm clock going off. Moaning in agony, he rolled over and bumped into a warm male body. Blinking his eyes, he smiled in pleasure and dug under the covers to touch Billy's taut, muscular build. "Oh, I can *so* get used to this." Finding that enticing morning hard-on, Angel wrapped his fingers around it and gave it a long, slow stroke.

Instantly Billy's eyes opened.

"Hello," Angel giggled.

"Well, that's a nice way to wake up in the morning." Billy stretched his arms over his head. "Now, why can't they invent an alarm clock that does that?"

Angel giggled. "You need to go to the bathroom? Or?"

"No. You go right ahead." Billy threw off the covers and spread his legs.

Sitting up, Angel licked his lips as he began working Billy's cock. "Look at you. Billy, you are so incredible."

"I was thinking the exact same thing. Move the blanket. Let me see you."

Angel shoved off the covers, revealing his own erection. Billy stared at his cock while Angel jerked him off. Angel felt extremely flattered he turned Billy on so much.

Billy's eyes closed and his body tightened up. Lovely white milky spatters speckled Billy's chest and abdomen. As

Billy caught his breath, Angel climbed over the top of him and wriggled on him, smearing the come between them.

Groaning in pleasure, Billy spread his legs wide, allowing Angel to lie between them. Angel began poking at Billy's back door. "Knock, knock, can I come in?"

"The door's open, gorgeous," Billy laughed.

Sitting up eagerly, Angel located the supplies he needed in the nightstand, then slid a rubber on quickly, followed by lube. Bending Billy's knees back, Angel pushed in, shivering in ecstasy. When he opened his eyes, Angel found Billy staring at him, a loving, but serious expression on his face. Quickening his thrusts, Angel gripped Billy's knees and pumped in deeply, coming and gasping as he did. Taking a moment to recover, Angel then pulled out, discarded the rubber and collapsed back down on Billy's chest. Both their hearts pounding as one, strong and powerful, Angel closed his eyes and savored the feeling of being loved and protected. It had been a very long time coming. And he was glad it finally arrived.

Gently, Billy stroked Angel's hair, running his fingers through its length. "Angel?"

"Yes, lover?"

"I've taken two weeks off."

"Yes?"

"Can you take any time off?"

Angel raised his head to be able to see Billy's eyes. "You want me to close the shop?"

"Close it? Let Summer run it? Get her someone to help her run it?"

"Why? Were you thinking of going somewhere? I can't leave Oliver alone."

"We don't have to go anywhere far. Just some day trips. Maybe just spend some quality time together."

Toying with Billy's right nipple as he considered, Angel

179

then said, "Yes. You're right. I need some time off after this horrible ordeal."

Smiling in pleasure, Billy wrapped around him and hugged him tight. "I adore you, Angel, so much."

His heart exploding in joy, Angel squirmed in excitement on Billy as he replied coyly in a tease, "Oh, Detective Sharpe, you say all the right things."

When Angel stepped out of the shower with Billy, Oliver shouted his name.

"What?" Angel poked his head out of the bathroom, a towel wrapped around his hips.

"Grandpa is on the phone," Oliver said, cupping his hand over the receiver.

"Dad?" Angel gulped in shock. He grabbed the phone from his son and said, "Hello?"

"Gabriel?"

"Dad? What's wrong? Is Mom all right?" Angel looked behind him, knowing Billy was trying not to listen.

"I just called to see if you were all right."

Tilting his head in question, Angel asked, "Why?"

"There's an article in the paper that said you were involved with a stalker. It upset your mother and I quite a bit. Oliver explained some of it to me, but I wanted to hear it from you. You need anything?"

Still suffering from shock, Angel sat down on his bed with the towel around his hips. "Wow. I thought you guys had disowned me."

"Perhaps that was a rash decision. A lot of time has past since those days, Gabriel. Your mother and I were hoping we could somehow patch things up. Maybe Oliver could spend some time with us. You know. To give you some time to recover from your ordeal."

Wiping at a tear, Angel looked up to see Billy standing in the doorway. Angel reached out his hand and Billy took it, sitting next to him on the bed. "Yes, Dad. That would be fantastic. I do need a break. I haven't had a proper vacation in almost ten years. Since Katherine died."

"Why don't you stop by? Are you working in the shop today?"

"I was planning on it. But I can come over after work."

"That's fine, son. Bring Oliver over for dinner."

"Uh, Dad…" Angel looked directly into Billy's eyes for courage.

"Yes, Gabriel?"

"I…I have a man in my life." Angel waited.

"Yes?"

"He…he's the detective that saved my life. His name is Billy Sharpe."

"Would you like to bring him over with you?"

"If that's okay."

"Yes. We're indebted to him for helping you. So, we'll see you later?"

"Around six?" Angel asked.

"Great. I'm looking forward to it, son."

"Thanks, Dad. Me, too." Angel hung up, then began crying, but they were tears of joy. "I can't believe it. My dad read an article about the incident in the paper, and he wants us to get together again. He wants to meet you. I haven't spoken to my dad in more than a decade. I'm floored, Billy."

"Aw, come here." Billy hugged him and rubbed his back warmly. "I'm very happy for you, Angel."

Angel sat back, saying, "I didn't think to ask you first. Is it all right? Do you want to come to my parents' house tonight for dinner?"

"Anything you want." Billy dabbed at Angel's tears with

his fingertips.

"They said they would take care of Oliver so I can take a break."

"Fantastic. Perfect timing."

A feeling overwhelmed Angel. Covering his face he sobbed into his hands for a moment, almost as if the relief was too much.

"Shh, baby, don't cry." Billy cupped his hands over Angel's.

Angel revealed his face, then whispered, "I can't remember a time in my life where everything worked out. I'm not used to it."

Billy started laughing. "Well, don't get used to it. Life ain't never what you expect, gorgeous."

A light knock was heard at the door. Angel told Oliver to come in.

"Are we seeing Grandma and Grandpa?" he asked.

"Yes. Tonight. You okay with that?"

"Yeah! Cool!" Oliver smiled.

"Look, Oliver," Angel began, "if Billy and I want to take some time off—"

"Yes," Oliver replied.

"Yes? You don't even know what I'm going to ask you."

"I do. You want to take a vacation with Billy. I can stay with Grandma and Grandpa. It's okay. You deserve it, Dad. After what you've been through."

Angel's eyes widened in awe. He reached out and said to his son, "Get over here!"

Closing the gap between them, Oliver allowed his father to hug him.

Feeling Billy wrapping around both of them, Angel began laughing, "Group hug!"

Hearing Oliver crack up was worth its weight in gold to Angel. They parted and giggled at each other. "Fine. Get ready for school, Oliver," Angel warned playfully.

"Okay. I can't wait to tell everyone about Perry's death!"

Before Angel could reply, Oliver had dashed out of his room. Angel looked over at Billy, who just shrugged innocently. "Kids." Billy threw up his hands.

"Get over here," Angel purred, then leapt over Billy and pinned him back on the mattress playfully.

Chapter Fourteen

Under the shade of an umbrella on a hot sandy beach in Gran Canaria, Billy stared through his sunglasses as a fantastic male emerged from the ocean water, walking naked towards him. That strut, the lean legs, the long brown, wet hair streaming down his neck and shoulders, he was an icon for a generation. Millions had salivated over that body, that face, and his enticing charisma. Perhaps future generations would never know who he was. But for him, Angel was everything. Shading his eyes as Angel Loveday stood dripping in front of him, Billy knew every person on that nude beach was admiring his perfect figure.

"Hey, copper," Angel purred seductively, "come here often?"

"I should arrest you. Being that incredibly gorgeous should be a crime."

"I can see your hard-on. Naughty boy."

"How the hell can I not be hard? Look at you."

"We can be naked, but we can't do rude things...too bad." Angel put his hands on his hips, pushing out his pelvis to taunt Billy.

"That's all I need. Arrested in the Canary Islands. My captain has had enough trouble with me."

"Want to come in for a swim?"

"I better. I can't sit with this thing hard all day." Billy tossed his glasses on the lounge chair, then reached out for Angel's hand. They walked down the silky white sand to the cresting waves. Diving in, spearing through the surf, Billy popped up and looked for Angel. Feeling him near, under the water, Billy waited as Angel surfaced directly in front of him. Wrapping around him lovingly, Billy kissed him, whispering, "I love you, Angel."

"And I love you, Billy."

They kissed passionately in the waves savoring the promise of a calm, perfect future together.

At the cottage, miles away, on the coast of California, a deliveryman exited his truck. After ringing the bell and receiving no answer, he set the bouquet down in front of the door and left.

On the card read, "Love you, Loveday. From your secret admirer."

The End

About the Author

Award-winning author G. A. Hauser was born in Fair Lawn, New Jersey, USA, and attended university in New York City. She moved to Seattle, Washington where she worked as a patrol officer with the Seattle Police Department. In early 2000 G.A. moved to Hertfordshire, England where she began her writing in earnest and published her first book, *In the Shadow of Alexander*. Now a full-time writer in Ohio, G.A. has written dozens of novels, including several best-sellers of gay fiction. For more information on other books by G.A., visit the author at her official website at:

www.authorga.com.

The G.A. Hauser Collection

Available Now
Single Titles

Unnecessary Roughness

The Physician and the Actor

For Love and Money

The Kiss

Naked Dragon

Secrets and Misdemeanors

Capital Games

Giving Up the Ghost

To Have and To Hostage

Love you, Loveday

The Boy Next Door

When Adam Met Jack

Exposure

The Vampire and the Man-eater

Murphy's Hero

Mark Antonious deMontford

Prince of Servitude

Calling Dr. Love

The Rape of St. Peter

The Wedding Planner

Going Deep

Double Trouble
Pirates
Miller's Tale
Vampire Nights
Teacher's Pet
In the Shadow of Alexander
The Rise and Fall of the Sacred Band of Thebes

The Action Series

Acting Naughty
Playing Dirty
Getting it in the End
Behaving Badly
Dripping Hot

Men in Motion Series

Mile High
Cruising
Driving Hard
Leather Boys

Rescue Series

Man to Man
Two In Two Out
Top Men

G.A. Hauser
Writing as Amanda Winters

Sister Moonshine
Nothing Like Romance
Silent Reign
Butterfly Suicide
Mutley's Crew

Coming Soon
Single Titles

All Man
Heart of Steele
It Takes a Man
Got Men?
In The Dark and What Should Never Be, Erotic Short Stories
Mark and Sharon (formerly titled A Question of Sex)

Made in the USA
Lexington, KY
07 October 2011